I0714644

Cirrus Stratus

Shome Dasgupta

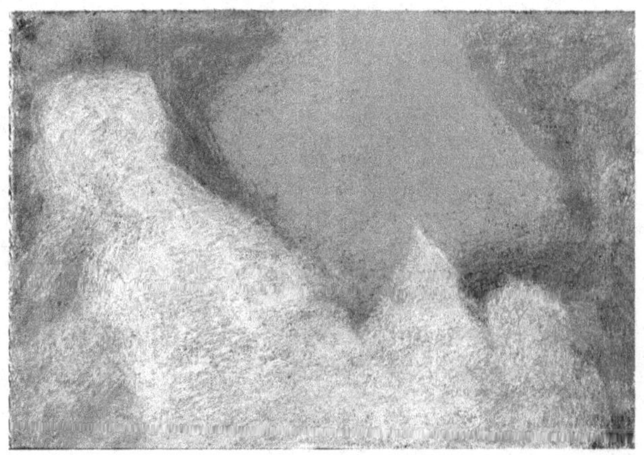

SPUYTEN DUYVIL
New York City

© 2022 Shome Dasgupta
ISBN 978-1-956005-80-6

cover art: t thilleman

Library of Congress Cataloging-in-Publication Data

Names: Dasgupta, Shome, author.
Title: Cirrus stratus / Shome Dasgupta.
Description: New York City : Spuyten Duyvil, [2022]
Identifiers: LCCN 2022030161 | ISBN 9781956005806 (paperback)
Subjects: LCGFT: Novels.
Classification: LCC PS3604.A826 C57 2022 | DDC 813/.6--dc23/eng/20220624
LC record available at https://lccn.loc.gov/2022030161

for Karl & Mandy

Before Cirrus Stratus's exile from the forgotten town of Dormier, he shot two horses for Vienna, the woman he had loved since the day of her birth. He had been watching over her from a distance, an untouchable guardian angel of sorts. Vienna had only seen him once during that span, when she had opened her eyes for the first time and saw the blurry figure of a very young Cirrus Stratus peering over the water trough at the town square. When he saw her eyes, Cirrus Stratus walked away, across the fields, past the market to his mother's hut in a community where only the untouchables lived. There, he made his first of 264 gifts for Vienna. The first one was a kite he had made using the spokes from a bicycle he had stolen and a shawl belonging to his mother, Alcee Vase Stratus.

Without her knowing, Cirrus Stratus found ways to present Vienna with gifts as she grew older—he stole chocolate, vases, wine, scarves, bread, cheese—and when he didn't steal, he made presents out of items he had taken throughout his life, making dolls out of lumber from construction sites, or necklaces using coal and silver taken from the blacksmith, or he would use scraps found in the junkyard to make shiny trinkets put together with glue and tape and candle wax.

Vienna never questioned where the gifts came from, as many suitors brought gifts to her in person or left them at the door while she was sleeping. Vienna and her mother, Sari Vendrellieu, were considered to be the dearest of the untouchables. Because of the mother's gentility and caring nature, they weren't scorned by the town like the other untouchables, and as Vienna's beauty grew, she had the city singing about her. Not only were the untouchables amazed by her beauty and affection, but all of Dormier ventured to the outskirts of the city to offer her gifts or to hear the softness of her voice.

Alejo Augestine was Vienna's most well-known suitor—it was no secret that he was in love with her, as he stayed up late at every Sunday night outside of the Vendrellieus' hut playing the Spanish guitar while surrounded by candles he had made by the local chandler. A prominent lawyer in the town of Dormier, Alejo had been a sought after bachelor by several women who found him to be both handsome and a gentleman, but Alejo didn't give them any attention—he was only thinking of one lady. He hoped that his own status in society would help Vienna to leave the untouchables and live a rich life full of silk and wool and decadent dishes and aged wine.

Cirrus Stratus was well aware of Alejo's pursuit of the beloved Vienna; sometimes his jealousy would get the best of him and he would wreck his own body by slamming himself against concrete walls or cutting himself. Sometimes Cirrus Stratus would get his revenge on Alejo by sneaking out to his house and breaking his porch lights or windows, or he would steal his flowers from the front garden or paint offensive words on his carriage. His mother talked to him about it and while Cirrus Stratus was passionate about his love for Vienna, she would not condone his actions, always telling him to be a gentleman, a strong man. Cirrus Stratus loved his mother—he would talk to her about his every thought, constantly learning from her, and he took her advice seriously. It wasn't that he didn't want to listen to his mother, but when it came to Vienna, his natural instincts took over. Alcee knew this, too, and she was at a loss as to how to fix it.

I've heard that Alejo's front yard has been covered with dead pigeons, Alcee said. She looked at Cirrus Stratus, who was sharpening a pencil. He didn't look at his mother but nodded his head.

It is a shame, Alcee said. He is a gentleman—someone I wish you could look up to as a model. Not like your father.

He's no longer my father, Cirrus Stratus said. And yes, it was me.

Do you think Vienna can love a man who kills pigeons? Alcee asked.

Cirrus Stratus stopped sharpening his pencil and scratched the charcoal against his chin.

It is all for her, Cirrus Stratus said. I'm trying, trying severely.

Wash the back of your neck, Alcee said.

Whether it was pigeons or donkeys or dogs, Cirrus Stratus couldn't stop himself from harassing Alejo's front yard. Alejo had put up reward signs for anyone who would tell him about the vandalism of his yard. No one said anything—no one could say anything because Cirrus Stratus, much like the town raccoons, was a master of stealth. Though his mother did not like his ways with dealing with Alejo, she did admire her son's intelligence and diligence. His obstinacy worried her but she knew that his stubbornness was not his fault—he had gotten it from her.

During Starry Night, the yearly festival celebrating the sky, Cirrus Stratus hid behind an oak tree next to the pavilion where the anniversary was taking place. He saw Vienna sitting at a table sipping a glass of wine and eating a green salad dressed with olive oil and almonds. Cirrus Stratus thought about going up to her to introduce himself. He thought about telling her that it was he who had left those gifts at the door of her hut. He thought about confessing his love to her. Cirrus Stratus licked his palms and rubbed his head, trying to fix his hair. He spat on his palms again and rubbed his chin and his forehead making sure any dirt from his earlier visit to the junkyard was gone. He fixed his shirt and pants and rubbed off any charcoal or bird excrement stains.

The night sky was lit with fireworks as the town gathered and drank and ate and danced. During the middle of the show, one firework exploded into solid dark blue sparks, making the moon look like the ocean, reminding Cirrus Stratus of his days spent on the cliff overlooking the water. He looked at Vienna under the splashes of exploding colors and saw the eyes he saw when she was born on the town square 22 years ago. Cirrus Stratus couldn't make himself move amidst the cracking sounds of the sky and the surrounding smoke smelling of gunpowder. He cursed himself as he saw Alejo bow before her and kiss the knuckles of her right hand. He listened to their conversation during the gaps of silence as the fireworks would go off every five minutes.

I have two of the most beautiful horses for you, Alejo said.

He lifted up his glass of wine and clinked it against Vienna's—the quiet toast made Cirrus Stratus angry. He kept hearing his mother's voice in his head, telling him to stay calm—telling him to be a gentleman.

You are too sweet, Vienna said.

The lines in Cirrus Stratus's forehead relaxed as Vienna spoke, her words soothing.

Vienna and Alejo looked up to see another round of fireworks, but Cirrus Stratus kept his eyes on Vienna. He spat at the roots of the oak and scratched his forearm.

Now tell me, Vienna said. What am I to do with these horses?

Groom them and love them, Alejo said. They are soft and gentle, like you.

Alejo put his hand on Vienna's and looked into her eyes.

I have heard of your love for these beautiful animals, he said. This is my pleasure.

Thank you, Vienna said. But that is too much. I have no place to keep them, as you know.

Alejo nodded his head—Cirrus Stratus could see his white teeth. He ran his tongue over his own and tasted the grit.

Come to my place tomorrow morning, Alejo said. Come see them. Come see where I live and maybe then you'll find a place to take care of them.

Are you asking for my union? Vienna answered.

There was a loud cheer from the crowd as the fireworks were at the height of their explosion. They formed umbrellas in the sky. Cirrus Stratus snuck in a bit closer but he could no longer hear the words spoken between Vienna and Alejo. They stood up and walked toward the crowd. Cirrus Stratus cursed and took the glass that Vienna had left on the table and tucked it into his pants. He left the party and went back to the hut where his mother was playing the violin, one of the few remnants she had from the past.

You are crazy, Alcee said.

Keep playing, mother, Cirrus Stratus replied.

Alcee continued to twist her bow around the strings, moving her head left and right, her eyes closed.

Your music is our own fireworks, Cirrus Stratus said.

He fell asleep to the playing of his mother's violin and he woke up early the next day. Alcee was still sleeping. The rooster at the adjacent hut was crowing and as the sun was rising, Cirrus Stratus put on his best clothes—clothes he had stolen from the nearby tailor. There were missing buttons, torn pockets, and uneven sleeves, but they were still more fashionable than his own clothes. He put on a brown vest with matching slacks. His bowtie wasn't tight and proper but he thought it looked fine, and his brown coat was oversized, but Cirrus Stratus didn't like tightly fitting clothes anyhow. He made his mother breakfast as she slept—a bowl of berries, toast and butter, and a small bit of bacon from a pig he had taken from a farm two weeks before. It was the last of the bacon, and Cirrus Stratus smiled as he put the plate on Alcee's bedside table, knowing that this was the best bacon he had ever made.

Alcee was famous for her thin neck—her black hair went down to her hips, and the beauty of her light brown skin had made the citizens of Dormier wish that they were a part of the untouchables. Everyone adored her except for her husband, previously known as Leaus Perdu III but now known as Lash Gorge Stratus, who was notorious for striking fear in the souls of those who hear even the slightest reference to his name—Lash Gorge Stratus—the man who allegedly shoved vegetables down the throats of those who had crossed him. He, too, became an untouchable after his falling out with Alcee, but managed to find his way into politics, spreading corruption and panic.

Cirrus Stratus wasn't always a part of that shunned group. He came from a wealthy family—his father, Leaus Perdu III, this was before he changed his name to Lash Gorge Stratus, was a well-known bowler not only in Dormier but around the world. His sponsors would provide the funding so that he could travel across the Pacific to Asia and attend the World Championships, where he had won the prize seven times in Japan, thus holding the record for winning the tournament as many times as there are days in the week. He was a Dormier hero, always applauded as he entered the market wearing his collar up and his signature wristband of leather and sparkling gems.

The Stratus Mansion was built in a crater of a deteriorating volcano hidden in a valley—land bought by the Stratus as soon as they arrived in the city centuries ago by boat.

Arriving with no money, Leaus Perdu III's grandparents through his father's side—Leaus Perdu and his wife Anita Alice Perdu—made their way by selling their cooking for land, and bit by bit, with the help of eggplant and chocolate, they were able to own most of the Dormier-Frasc Valley, which included the Dormier Volcano—it had become active only once during the lifespan of the grandparents. Despite his success, Leaus Perdu didn't forget his past and impoverished upbringing—nor did his son, Leaus Perdu II, whose gentle eyes had been known to make people cry from a certain sadness that came with the softness of his appearance. Leaus Perdu II, a bank owner and businessman who owned two cafes and the opera house, always kept to himself, and not too many people knew about him until his wife, Dimanche Fridatte Charon Perdu, had passed away as she bathed in the River of Blue. While wading in the water, a maple leaf tree had fallen over from the wind, knocking her down to the riverbed. Dimanche had no way out and drowned while tench fish circled around her trying to find a way to help her. One tried to give breath to her underwater but Dimanche kept her mouth closed and smiled. Before drowning, she had scratched into the bark of the maple leaf, Leaus Perdu II's name followed by, "The Sun Looks So Pretty Underwater."

Dimanche was well loved by the inhabitants of Dormier— she was seen as a matron of the city—sponsoring activities to help promote good energy around the town. She took care of the homeless and made yearly donations to the school to make sure that the students had all of the essential tools to get the best education. Dimanche realized that the people looked to her for support and encouragement and she took on the responsibility with a fervor of energy.

Her funeral was the first time the Dormierians could get to know Leaus Perdu II. He whispered his eulogy, addressing it only to the coffin. Those who attended still cried as they imagined his quiet words filtering through their ears. On that night of the funeral, Leaus Perdu II got a tattoo on his left forearm—it was Dimanche's last words written on the bark of the Maple Leaf.

With the death of his mother, Leaus Perdu III grew up with his father and grandfather's upbringing. He was humble at first and even his stardom related to his bowling didn't change his ways. During the end of his career, he was soon invited to join the politics of Dormier. He would be the first Stratus to do so, and despite the warnings of his father and grandfather, and despite his own hesitance at first, Leaus Perdu III joined the Ethicginian Party under the pressure of its leader, Abliss Rang. It was under Abliss's mentorship that Leaus Perdu III's eyes and demeanor changed from a sports hero and town leader to a soul full of scars and holes. The competitive energy overtook his humility as he became determined to keep the opposing party, the Principlists, from taking control of the city. His skin became rougher—his palms became calloused, not from his years of bowling, but from the constant scraping of his hands against his own frozen mind.

Alcee wouldn't tolerate Leaus Perdu III's antics. He became a completely different man, and he wasn't the person she once loved though Leaus Perdu III still possessed a strong passion for his wife. She left him, and Leaus Perdu III became bitter. She took Cirrus Stratus with her, as well as their belongings and left the valley to live a secluded life in the corner of the town, just off the coast, on a beach where only a few others lived. Before leaving, her last words to her husband were "Even strangers have a familiarity which you lack." Though Leaus Perdu III pleaded with her to stay, making her countless promises, Alcee didn't take the chance. She wanted Cirrus Stratus to live a life outside the world of Leaus Perdu III, and it was then that Leaus Perdu III became darker and darker and found himself in a world full of violence and power. He became Lash Gorge Stratus.

Under Lash Gorge Stratus's scorn, he commissioned his party to ransack the dwellings of his wife and the others who were living on the beach. His gang destroyed their houses, stole their belongings, and set the ocean on fire. Alcee and Cirrus Stratus found themselves living with the untouchables, going from silk saris and fresh fruit to orange peels and scraps of cloth found in the junkyard. They had lived a life made of gold, and now they were living a life full of rust.

It was here, with the untouchables, where Cirrus Stratus fell in love as he was trying to steal copper cups from the saloon. While he was crawling through the back entrance, he heard a loud scream and turned around, peering over the water trough to see Sari wearing a long blue gown pulled up to her thighs, and her legs spread apart. As Vienna was born, silent and curious—her arms reaching out toward the sky, her eyes open for the first time—Cirrus Stratus knew he was in love. It was the feeling his mother would talk to him about when she talked about Leaus Perdu III before he had turned into a different man. Kites, Cirrus Stratus had thought and immediately ran back to his hut to make his favorite toy for Vienna.

Alcee opened her eyes.

Sleep mother, Cirrus Stratus said. And then eat.

Alcee took a deep breath and ate a berry.

This is the last of the bacon, she said. You take it. I won't let you steal anymore pigs.

I won't, Cirrus Stratus said. And no, you eat. Look at my gut—I've had plenty of bacon during the past two weeks.

Nonsense, son, Alcee said. Your gut is the size of a firstborn pup. And your bones are showing and your eyes are sinking.

Prim and proper, Cirrus Stratus said. I'm going for a morning walk. I'll be back before tea to finish the chores.

The rooster continued to crow.

The morning song is delightful, Alcee said.

Dormier was quiet following the Starry Night—the town was recouping from the party which had gone well into the early morning, but Cirrus Stratus knew that Alejo was a man who strictly followed his routines. Every Sunday he would take one of his horses and trot around town, gloating about his wealth. On that Sunday after the Starry Night, Cirrus Stratus had assumed correctly, as Alejo was on his horse, traveling around town, and he snuck in from the back, crawling through the acres of land toward the barn.

There were four horses in the stable—two brown and two black. Cirrus Stratus walked up to the first horse —its head was lowered, eyes looking at Cirrus Stratus. He ran his hand along the back of its night, whispering and humming. The horse made a gentle grunt and pushed its head against Cirrus Stratus's hands, and he continued to pet it.

I don't know your name, he said. I am Cirrus Stratus the Untouchable. I have dreamt about you before.

The horse slowly rocked its head back and forth. The smell of manure made Cirrus Stratus lick his lips.

I shall name you, he said. I shall name you Llama, and you will be loved, no matter what happens.

Cirrus Stratus moved on to the next horse—a black one, shinier than Llama and more active in the stables.

I shall name you Vespasiano.

Vespasiano moved back and forth, trying to turn its body around.

Cirrus Stratus tickled the back of the black horse's ear.

You will be free, he said.

He took two carrots from a sack between the two horses and fed them both. He went to the other two horses and unlocked their stables, patting them on their sides.

Go, Cirrus Stratus said. Leave here and seek the sky. The two horses trotted out of the barn. He took two saddles and strapped his new friends, tying a rope from Llama to Vespasiano. Saddling the black horse, Cirrus Stratus lightly tapped his heels against its side and they left the barn and trotted across the acres.

Cirrus Stratus took them to one of his hiding spots—a

place he would seek when he knew someone was chasing him after committing thievery or getting in a fight or getting in trouble for throwing rocks at the houses of the rich.

The sunlight struck the back of his head as Cirrus Stratus looked up toward the sky and closed his eyes. The soft thuds of the horses' hooves were lulling him to sleep—by the time they left Alejo's acres, he had fallen in love with both horses. He guided them into a thickly wooded parcel of land, full of green and wildlife. He found the path he had made years ago when fleeing from a chimney sweeper after stealing his eyeglasses because he wanted to use the frames to break into the baker's shop. Llama and Vespasiano strolled with ease, showing a sense of comfort with their new guide. Cirrus Stratus let the leaves brush against his face—he pulled twigs off the bark of the kapoks and ran them across the backs of the two horses. He heard the sounds of the river, the whirring of the water as it traveled toward the ocean. There came the opening—a cul-de-sac bordered by the river and a series of prostrate trees which Cirrus Stratus had cut down in an effort to build a shelter of some sort when he was hiding in the rain.

He went to a mound of broken branches and shrubs and dug through the middle of it, pulling out a rusted rifle, brown and orange and caking away. He didn't steal the rifle—he found it at the junkyard the day after Shakur Velli had shot his wife's lover four years ago. Shakur was the local jeweler, a highly regarded gentleman. One night he caught his wife, Asuri Eloide Velli, on her knees in the sitting room with Belizaire Hondre, an egg farmer. Asuri did not speak as she saw her husband walking in wearing his monocle and holding a swan made of diamonds. Shakur walked past Asuri and Belizaire and put the swan on the mantle before going to the cabinet in the bedroom. He returned holding his rifle and aimed it at Belizaire.

I will have fresh eggs in the morning, Belizaire said.

Shakur shot him two times in the head and he dropped to the floor in front of Asuri. She stood up, still silent, staring at the swan on the mantle.

You look beautiful, Shakur said. I made the swan for you. Good sand.

Those were his last words before Shakur disappeared, never to be seen again in Dormier, and since that night, Asuri had become a hermit. When her friends would try to visit her, they would see her through the window, sitting near the mantle and staring at the swan, mumbling to herself.

Cirrus Stratus aimed the rifle at Llama, who looked at him with lowered eyes. She gave a gentle grunt and shuffled about to where the side of her head faced Cirrus Stratus.

This is all for love, said Cirrus Stratus. Forgive me and I will make it up to you when I am gone.

He reloaded and pulled the trigger. He aimed the rifle at Vespasiano, who lifted her head and faced Cirrus Stratus.

I will see you some time, Cirrus Stratus said. Vienna Vienna.

The two horses lay dead in the woods. After the echoes of the shots had quieted, the sound of the river took over. Cirrus Stratus went up to each horse, his eyes watery and round. He whispered to them.

I'm sorry, Cirrus Stratus said. I am not a good man. I am not a man at all.

He put the rifle back into the mound and straightened his shirt and slacks. He washed his face in the river and left to go home.

On the same day that Cirrus Stratus had shot Alejo's two horses, Vienna had accepted Alejo's invitation to see Llama and Vespasiano. Alejo dressed in his finest clothes—his thinned mustache trimmed and subtle—and he wore his newest top hat which he had made specifically for the occasion. Vienna, herself, did not particularly want to go even though she had a passion for the beauty of horses. She did not know what to think about her main suitor; she only knew that he was a gentleman. It was under Sari's persuasion that she accepted the invitation.

He is a nice young man, Sari said. I do not see why you shouldn't visit him. He has shown nothing but love and care for you.

But what good is love if I don't reciprocate it? Vienna wondered aloud.

A tragedy, her mother said.

I do not want to lead him on, Vienna said. You've always told me to be true and honest and to never lie to any bird or caterpillar.

But that does not mean you should be unkind and uncaring, Sari said. Look at Lash Gorge Stratus. Would you not say he is an honest man? He speaks openly and does whatever he wants to do with no regrets. But he is ruthless. A killer and a scoundrel.

The once adored hero of Dormier, her daughter said. Now an untouchable, scorned and scorning.

The first untouchable to hold office, Sari said.

Vienna wrapped herself in a green and orange shawl

and wore her red and black sandals—the straps covered in gems. She had received them as a gift from Cirrus Stratus but had assumed they were given to her by Alejo.

Alejo opened the door and bowed as he saw Vienna standing in front of him.

Please, Vienna said. Such a gesture is not for an untouchable but it is very much appreciated.

You are definitely untouchable, Alejo said, but not in the manner you speak of.

Alejo offered her tea and biscuits but Vienna politely declined, ignoring his joke.

I can't stay for too long, she said. I must help my mother tend to her business.

Soon you all won't have to worry about any of that, Alejo said.

Vienna reluctantly laughed and followed Alejo out into the acres behind his mansion.

Your mother works hard, Alejo said. I hear she is the best cook in your area.

She's also a great seamstress, Vienna said.

That's right, Alejo said. And what about yourself? What would you like to do if you could do anything you wanted?

He walked close to her side, not noticing Vienna's attempt to keep some space between them.

I haven't any time to think about that, Vienna said. I can only dream of what to do tomorrow. One day at a time.

Soon, Alejo said, your dreams will have no limitations.

Alejo opened the door to the stable and saw that his two horses weren't there. He looked out onto the field and saw nothing.

What is this? Alejo said. Where are my horses? Excuse me, *your* horses.

He shouted his servant's name and Thuroon soon appeared holding a bucket of soapy water. He tried hard not to stare at Vienna but he could not help but to adore her brown skin and eyes. Vienna lowered her head and smiled.

Namaste, Thuroon said. He bowed.

Vienna put her hands together and returned the gesture.

Alejo was conveying a different emotion. His scrunched forehead and narrow eyes and tucked in cheeks finally caught Thuroon's attention.

Sir, Thuroon said. I have not tended to the horses since we were last here together grooming them.

Did you not lock the gates? Alejo said.

Thuroon knew that it was Alejo who was supposed to lock the gates, as he had been told to leave and tend to the front garden before the sun came down. Alejo was the one who was last at the stables. He also knew not to expose Alejo in front of the lady he was pursuing.

Sir, Thuroon said. I cannot remember.

Idiot, Alejo said. Go. Find the horses. If you don't find them, don't come back.

Vienna sighed and looked at Alejo.

My dear, Alejo said. I'm so sorry you had to witness this but I must stay strict. If I don't, look what happens. Your gifts—they are gone.

Vienna didn't respond but bowed her head toward Thuroon and put her hands together. Thuroon did the same and ran off to find Alejo's horses.

This is an embarrassment, Alejo said.

Please, Vienna said. This anger is all for naught. It won't bring the horses back.

Your wisdom, Alejo said, is another quality that makes you beautiful like a marigold in full bloom under the shadow of the sun.

Please, Vienna said. Your words are much appreciated, but I must go now.

Stay, Alejo said.

My mother is waiting for me, she insisted.

Stay, Alejo said. Please let me make up for this embarrassment—have dinner with me. There is tandoori and lamb being made just for you. No offense to your mother, but my chef—he is the best in town.

Vienna admired Alejo's confidence and thoughtfulness but she still did not have any kind of feelings for him. She did think about it one night, the idea of being rich and not having to worry about the everyday chores and tasks just for shelter and food but still, her current lifestyle prevailed over a life with Alejo.

I'm sure he is the best, Vienna said, as I can only assume to expect the best.

That is why I look to you, Alejo said. Come with me. Let us talk about your mother. Perhaps we can think of a way for her to come work for me.

For you, Vienna repeated, stunned.

She fixed her shawl, wrapping it tighter against her skin as the winds were coming in. She looked out in the field and saw Thuroon running into the forest.

I have offended you, Alejo said. That was not my intention.

What are your intentions? Vienna asked.

Your love, he said. Your love—to give you the world.

But what if I don't want the world?

Then your naivety has the better of you, Alejo said.

He immediately apologized.

The loss of horses has brought out the worst in me, he stuttered.

That is good, Vienna said. For how can we truly know someone when we haven't seen one's worst? And if this is the reason to make you as such, then I must say, your problems are nothing but a pinch of salt.

Vienna made her way out of the stables.

Please, Alejo said, trying not to show his tears.

My words were without thought, Alejo pleaded. Thuroon knows that he can still work for me. We do this all the time.

I must go, Vienna said.

Let my driver take you, Alejo said.

I will walk, Vienna said. My legs have no limits.

She took off her sandals.

Here, Vienna said. Thank you so much for the sandals, but please, out of decency, take them back. And please, no more.

Pretty, Alejo said, but those are not from me.

My blessing, Vienna said.

She put them back on and without saying another word to Alejo, Vienna left his place and started walking back to her hut. She heard faintly in the background shots being fired, coming from the beyond the forest. Alejo knew not to plead with her anymore and watched her as she walked away.

A shame, Alejo said. Such beauty and yet she sticks to the caked pots of the untouchables.

When Vienna reached her home, it was dark, and the streets were lit by the small fires in front of each hut—some used them for cooking, while others for warmth. Sari was sitting at the table with thread, sewing a blue and pink sari as a gift to one of her neighbors for always supporting her business. Vienna, without speaking, walked straight to the corner of the room to sleep on a patchy rug.

Time to dream, Sari said.

She could tell by her daughter's antics that the visit didn't go well.

There are no dreams, Vienna said. Mother, my dream is your dream.

Then dream of chocolate and horses, Sari said.

She spit on the needle and wiped it clean before threading it.

Look, she said. You have a letter.

Vienna had never received a letter before—she stayed on the rug staring at the envelope jutting over the table. She had received a countless number of gifts, but never a letter, and the inherently personal nature of a handwritten note made her hesitant. She asked about its source.

There was a knock and when I came out, but no one was there, and this envelope was at my feet, Sari said. Perhaps Alejo.

It can't be, Vienna said. That is done with.

Vienna didn't move from her corner, and Sari handed her the envelope. It was covered in dirt and the handwriting on the envelope itself was illegible. It smelled of mud. She opened it.

It's a map, Vienna said.

To where? Sari asked. To all of the treasures of the world?

It looks like it leads to a place near the river, Vienna said. Where a cul-de-sac forms.

Sari told her not to go—that it sounded dangerous and the forest was too unknown to explore, either alone or with company, and Vienna agreed. She didn't mention to her mother the writing at the bottom of the map which read, "I am sorry I did this for you. I cannot control my feelings. Say no to him."

Him, Vienna realized, was a reference to Alejo, and she wondered who else would know about his invitation. Her curiosity led her to sneak out in the middle of the night, holding a small torch to guide her into the forest void of light. She found the path and followed along as the map had shown. The night sounds didn't scare Vienna but instead they comforted her, making her feel like she was not alone; however, along with the torch, she had tucked a dagger into the rim of her garment around her waist. It had become cold, and Vienna could see her breath with each step, and the heat from the torch was not enough, as her teeth shook and rattled with the cold.

She arrived at the cul-de-sac where the forest had opened up, and the area was lit by the bare sky—the moon shone through directly on top of the two dead horses. Around them, were a series of candles, and in between the two horses, was another envelope. Vienna covered her mouth and nose as the smell was too strong for her liking, and the wind in the open had magnified the stench. The sound of the river was mixed in with the cracking branches in the wind.

This cannot be for me, Vienna thought. Who would do such a horrendous action? How can this be a gift? The tears came down her face as she ran her hand on the flanks of each horse. Looking at the envelope, she saw her name written in perfect penmanship.

Vienna Vienna,

Even a kite with holes and torn edges can be flown into the endless by the touch of your fingers.

My name is Cirrus Stratus the Untouchable. One day you will love me, but never in the same way I love you.

There is no one else in this world but us. Our dreams of nothing and coal are what keep us going. Never change your dreams and never forget that where we come from has everything and nothing to do with where we'll be. One day we will dream together beside the ocean.

Your love for horses—these are for you. I am sorry they are dead—this is my doing. But aren't they beautiful even in their death? The beauty of truth. This is where we live—you are the grace these horses exhibit, and their death is the life you live. I cannot speak for myself. I have no beauty as you can see, but the death in life is my comforted fortune. Never fall in love with a pebble or a rock—both are deceptive. Only give attention to the dirt buried underneath your soul—this is where nothing bares all.

The letter ended with Cirrus Stratus's signature. Vienna ran as fast as she could through the forest, losing her torch and sandals on her way. She could make out by the light coming through the branches, the path leading back to familiar territory. She cried the whole time—her tears stinging her face in the cold. She ran without stopping once, breathing hard as she got back to her hut. Sari was sleeping. The fires along the street were out, and there was nothing but darkness and the loud heaving of Vienna's lungs. She stood outside until her breathing had calmed, still holding the letter from Cirrus Stratus. She walked in and went to her corner and closed her eyes, but she knew that it would lead to nowhere, and she was still awake when the rooster's first crow awakened the untouchables.

You look sick, Sari said.

She stood over her daughter, looking down at her. Her bare chest was still full and protruding. There was no question as to where Vienna had gotten her beauty but no one ever pursued Sari, knowing her history, her life of cold stone. She was a kind and gentle woman, but underneath her skin, the untouchables and the city of Dormier knew there was a past full of swollen ghosts. Vienna did not know her father and Sari only knew him for one night. Her boss at the time was Rabi Ankar Hosh The Peasant. Her only task was to persuade Rabi's potential customers, using her beauty and charm, into giving him money for a night with Sari. It was a game though, and as long as Sari was able to bring in money, he allowed Sari to play her games with his clients.

Sari would visit the local bars and alleys and parties, seducing men into taking her home for the night; however, it wasn't just a payment the clients needed to make. They would pay her first, but when they arrived at their homes—or inns for that matter—they had to be able to hold an intelligent conversation with Sari. They would need to answer her questions, and if they were unable to answer, then she kept the money and took it to Rabi. She would get her cut and move on to the next client. Of course, this led to some dangerous situations for Sari. In particular, there was one night with Alamar Horace, a well-known gambler who had strong ties to the Ethicginian Party. They would provide him with the funds to make his money through cards and roulette, and most of the time, he would triple or quadruple the original amount. He would keep a percentage of it and also make a donation to the Party, and both of them would be making a profit.

One drunken night, as Alamar was doing well at the wheel, Sari had decided to approach him, even though Rabi The Peasant warned her that she should stay away from him. Sari herself was on her ninth glass of wine and was feeling uninhibited that night, though she was not drunk. Her past lifestyle left her with a high tolerance of alcohol and drugs—this allowed her to gain more clients for Rabi.

Do you think you can handle me, Alamar Horace The Gambler? Sari asked.

Alamar looked at her with red eyes and grinned.

You will be my best bet, he replied.

He finished his game with one hand holding his bottle, and the other hand holding Sari's. They left the bar and walked upstairs to where the rooms were kept. The rooms were mostly small—one single-sized bed, one painting, one window, and one vase. Alamar opened the door to one room that was already occupied. Sari saw the bare of the lady's back humped over a full bellied man who still wore his glasses and top hat.

This room is reserved, the man said, breathing heavily and covered in sweat.

The lady shushed him and stood up. Sari nodded her head at her, and the lady did the same.

You have a lovely back, Sari said.

Nothing compared to yours, the lady replied.

She turned toward Alamar.

My apologies, the lady said. We will find another room.

This is absurd, the man said.

I will chop it off, Alamar said.

He pulled out his dagger.

The man stood up and wrapped himself in the blanket, grabbing his slacks and shirt.

My apologies, the man said.

The couple left the room but before leaving, the lady put her hand on Sari's shoulder.

To live, she said.

Death's patience, Sari said.

Alamar stumbled to the bed. I've been waiting for you for quite some time, he said.

Why didn't you ask me? Sari said.

I ask no one, Alamar said. Come—unwrap yourself and show me your spectacle.

It is not that easy, my friend, she said. Let us talk first.

Talk, he said. Your mouth is not made for talking.

You know how it works, Sari said.

Alamar sat up and lit a cigar.

Where are my manners? he puffed. Fine. Talk. I would like to be amused.

What are your thoughts on Odysseus when we find him by himself? Sari asked. How would you describe his character—his thoughts and actions reveal much when he is alone. Tell me.

Odysseus. . . Alamar said. Odysseus. . . .

Sari could tell Alamar had no clue about whom she was talking and moved on to the next question.

Dormier has been struggling economically for the past twenty years or for as long as I can remember, she said. How can the levels of poverty change? How can the untouchables be touchable? What are some strategies to help rectify this?

Alamar stood up and threw his cigar against the wall.

You speak poorly of the Ethicginian Party, he said. Such audacity. Such stupidity. The system is not set up for everyone, for everyone is not capable of living up to the system.

Your system is corrupt and flawed, Sari said.

She wasn't able to move on to the next question—Alamar's madness had taken over as he turned the bed over, and threw the vase against the window. Pieces of the window fell to the floor—the vase rolled around, intact. The inn couldn't afford glass vases—they were all made of stone taken from the limestone quarry.

Are you daring me to stab you? Alamar yelled.

He walked up to her and grabbed her by the shoulders. Sari didn't move. She stared directly into his eyes.

You lose, she said. I will take my money and leave.

Alamar slapped her. Sari, without hesitation, slapped him back.

Next time it will be a fist, Alamar said. No money. I am in no mood either. You're lucky.

Rabi will come after you, Sari said. You shouldn't disrespect him.

Rabi is a little pig, Alamar said. Tell him I will kill him. Go before I take out my dagger. He pushed her against the wall and walked out of the room. Sari waited awhile and went out the back way.

Rabi wasn't too pleased with Sari when he heard about what had happened the night before. She took a beating from him and he told her that if she messed up again, he would let the dogs loose on her.

The night that Vienna was conceived was quite different than her experience with Alamar. His name was Equador Las Veas—a scholarly man who studied metallurgy in Hungary. He was a distinguished academic and the most sought out consultant when it came to the art of ores. He was a musician, too—playing for a marching band during his tenure at Hungary. He played the drums.

That night when she met him at a soiree, Equador Las

Veas was immediately attracted to Sari but too shy to talk to her. He was never good in social situations, and the only reason why he was at the party was to entertain one of his colleagues from overseas. Sari was attracted to him as well, not for the potential money but by his eyes—she couldn't see through them. All she could see was the beach and the ocean waves rolling in toward her.

I haven't seen you here before, Sari said.

I've come here for a conference, Equador Las Veas said. I reside in Budapest—my work is there.

I hope you enjoy your stay here, Sari said.

Equador Las Veas opened his mouth to speak but he coughed instead.

Excuse me, he said. Let me pour you another glass. I'm sorry about that.

Sari followed him to the mini-bar and handed her glass to him. To Equador Las Veas's delight, his cough into Sari's glass had led to a conversation between the two. Sari was pleased, too, as they talked about drumming and philosophy and their favorite plays, which led to more discussions about the world and the arts and their relationships with the humanities.

Come with me, Sari said. I want to do something for you. To you.

Equador Las Veas looked around for his friend and saw him talking with a group of people, shouting and laughing.

I should stay by my friend, Equador Las Veas said. He's never been here before.

Sari looked at his friend and sipped her glass of red wine.

He doesn't look too uncomfortable, she said. Come. Let's go for a walk.

She took Equador Las Veas's hand and they went outside and made their way around town. He asked her about her profession, her family, and her interests, and Sari did well to steer him away from giving him too much information, though she wanted to tell him everything.

I love to sew, she said. I love to kiss the ocean as the sun rises. I love to love that which cannot be understood or held. Equador Las Veas took interest in her views and he listened to her with great attention, and for the first time, looked directly into her eyes as they walked down the pavement past closed stores and dimly lit houses.

You are untouchable, Equador Las Veas said.

Well, I *am* an untouchable, Sari said.

She realized what she had said—or confessed, rather—and stopped walking, waiting for Equador Las Veas's reaction. He smiled and kissed her knuckles.

You are untouchable, he repeated.

Sari hadn't shown any kind of sad sentiment since she first began living on the streets, trying to provide for herself. She tried hard to not let him see the three teardrops falling from her eyes but the moon shone directly on them. To take the attention away from the situation, both awkward for Sari, and naturally, as always, awkward for Equador Las Veas, he ran down the pavement doing cartwheels, and when he came to a stop, the dizziness made him stumble and fall to the ground. Sari rushed toward him, helping him stand up. Equador Las Veas was breathing hard.

This is where I live, Sari said.

She pointed to a makeshift hut which consisted of eight bamboo sticks—its walls were made of three thick rundown, half-torn afghans. Equador Las Veas ran his fingers down the woven cloth and looked up at the stars.

What do you do when the winter comes, Equador Las Veas said.

Shiver, Sari said.

At least you're shivering in a place you've built by your own hands, Equador Las Veas said. Not too many people have that skill.

Sari pushed the afghan aside and led him inside. She unwrapped herself, without saying a word. Equador Las Veas stood in front of her and watched, both amazed by her beauty and in shock that there was a nude lady standing in front of him.

I don't know what to do, Equador Las Veas said.

She unstrapped his suspenders and combed his hair back with her fingers. She unbuttoned his shirt and ran her palms down his chest until they got to his waist and she unbuttoned his pants. For once, Sari did not think about money or Rabi The Peasant. She thought about pure pleasure and closed her eyes, losing herself in Equador Las Veas's skin. She listened to his breathing and moaned in harmony, guiding his hands and lips, his body—at first, the movements were unnatural and hesitant but he eventually found a rhythm with the help of Sari's hands. He pushed against her lips and he felt the softness, and he pushed against her breasts and felt the softness, and he pushed against her hips and felt the hardness and Sari's home was full of carbon dioxide and both the innocence and experience of the two. This was the night Vienna was conceived—during the night they first felt the threads of love. The next morning, Equador Las Veas looked at Sari with watery eyes, and Sari bowed her head and kissed his chin. They didn't speak and Equador Las Veas left, walking and looking at the sun.

The roosters continued to crow as Vienna looked up at her mother—she couldn't stop thinking about the forest.

I just didn't sleep well, Vienna said.

Sari noticed her feet covered in dirt and mud. She could smell the forest in her but didn't say anything else. Her place, their place, was not the same makeshift hut where Sari was residing during her time with Rabi The Peasant. When she realized she was pregnant, she quit her job. Rabi The Peasant forbade her to, but Sari laughed in her face and spat at his feet. As she tried to leave, Rabi The Peasant grabbed her shoulder and tried to shake her, but Sari broke free and held a knife to his throat. Nothing else was said, and that was the last time they saw each other. Since then, Sari had done well to keep nourishment and shelter by sewing and cooking for the untouchables. There was soon a vacant space further down from where she was staying, and she moved there a day before Vienna was born. It was a two room hut made out of good clay. She decorated it with bits and pieces of what she could find, or with gifts from her neighbors, and it had become a place that Sari, and eventually Vienna, could find contentment.

She started to cook eggs and asparagus for the morning meal, and Vienna stayed in the corner with her eyes closed thinking about the two dead horses and the letter from the unknown.

When Leaus Perdu III was on the brink of breaking through the bowling world, he was a man of the family—always taking care of wife and son. He put his family before any other factor in his life, and when his bowling career took off, he made sure to give them extra attention, for Alcee and Cirrus Stratus couldn't travel with him due to the daily obligations at home. Although Alcee was happy for her husband's success, she found the sport boring, and traveling across the ocean to watch him play was not the ideal way to spend her days.

In between the tournaments, the Perdu family would frequent the park and fly kites, or they would go out for dinner or to the theater. This became harder and harder to do once his fame peaked, but it was never to the point that the family could not peacefully share their time with each other. Though he was shy toward his fans, he also realized the role he played in their lives, for Dormier barely existed anymore since the explosion of Dormier Volcano had almost destroyed the city in its entirety. In its effort to rebuild itself, Leaus Perdu III played a crucial role in spreading a positive vibe throughout the city and beyond.

On one Sunday, Leaus Perdu III took his son far into the valley upon an elevated open area where the wind was strong and the seabirds flew with perfect feathers. Cirrus Stratus was six years old then—the age where his eyes were full of wonder and curiosity. All he knew then was chocolate and freshly squeezed lemon juice. This was the first time Cirrus Stratus flew a kite. His father would tell him to hold the handle and he would pick his son up and start running until it caught the wind. As Leaus Perdu III set him down, Cirrus Stratus didn't have strength to control the kite, and he himself started to lift off the ground, looking back at his father who stood there with an open mouth and raised eyebrows.

Where am I going father? he asked.

He was twirling in the air, with his feet barely scraping the rock below him.

Keep going, Leaus Perdu III said. Let the sky be your map to the universe.

Cirrus Stratus continued to elevate and the kite had its own life; it was steering him in every direction. Soon he found himself with the seabirds, and his father's head was just a spot in the rock. The cold air made his eyes water, and the wind beating against his face stung. Cirrus Stratus shouted—he did not know why—for out of joy or fear, he continued to shout. As the kite lowered, caught in an air trap, Leaus Perdu III got hold of his son and told him to let go of the kite. Upon release, the green fabric soared toward the sun—a seabird took it in its beak and flew until it had disappeared from their sight.

Leaus Perdu III put his hand on his son's shoulder—Cirrus Stratus breathed hard, wiping the tears from his frozen face.

I was almost gone father, Cirrus Stratus said.

What did you see? Leaus Perdu III asked.

I saw the magma in the sun's core, he said. I saw the sleeping stars waiting to wake up.

Always remember what you saw, his father said, putting

his son over his shoulders. Always remember that feeling when you were swimming with the clouds. No one can take that away from you.

That was the only good memory Cirrus Stratus had of his father. Leaus Perdu III, before he became Lash Gorge Stratus, had the same relationship with his own father. Leaus Perdu II's gentility and love for his family had a strong influence early on in Leaus Perdu III's life.

His fondest memory of Leaus Perdu II was when he was sitting on his lap in the library of their house—the smell of tobacco pipe mixed in with the perfume of his late mother which Leaus Perdu II would dab on his neck every week since the passing of his wife. Leaus Perdu III listened to his father's stories about Dimanche. Leaus Perdu III was four when his mother died in the River Of Blue and certain memories existed only through his father's tranquil voice.

Every night she would sprinkle pepper under her pillow, Leaus Perdu II said. She loved to sneeze in the morning. She loved to rub her eyes as the sun rose.

He puffed on his cherry red pipe and rubbed his forehead, staring at the leather bound books in his library. Leaus Perdu III tapped his fingers on his father's knees as he listened, pretending to play the piano.

She was a wonderful musician, his father said. The way you're pressing down on my knees—you got that from watching her, from listening to her, though you may not remember it.

I remember, Leaus Perdu III said.

Waltz #14, Leaus Perdu II said. She wrote that for our wedding day. The tears came as she played it.

Leaus Perdu III started to sing some of the words as he tried to remember her sitting at the piano in the recreation room. His son joined him and sang along. They sang about the moon and the thin and frail night, the song Dimanche would sing when she wanted to express the love she had for her husband.

You sing well, Leaus Perdu II said.

Early in Cirrus Stratus's youth, Leaus Perdu III would sing the same song to his son to help him go to sleep. Cirrus Stratus had nightmares—not the ones with monsters and beasts, but ones where he envisioned the death of his parents—constantly being stabbed by thick branches through their eyes and ears and mouths. It was this song that helped him dream about the grandmother he never knew.

The way she dressed, Leaus Perdu II said to his son. Wrapped in green and silver and blue fabrics. Her eyes— they were welcoming and comforting. The perfume you smell—it hypnotized anyone around her.

Leaus Perdu III put his nose to his father's neck and sniffed. His father lifted him up into the air and looked directly in his eyes.

Oh Leaus, Leaus Perdu II said. What will you become?

The greatest man mother would have known, he said. I will be the keeper of the night.

Come, Leaus Perdu II said. Your grandparents should be here soon. Let us set the table—just you and I and we will use the plates your mother made for you just before you were born.

Lash Gorge Stratus thought about that night as he sat on the stoop of a burning house behind him. He stroked his hand against the scar on his cheek and stared into the memories of his father. There were three other men there—his cohorts, who were continuing to pour gasoline along the flanks of the house and setting it on fire.

Burn it down until there is nothing left but the teeth of the dirt, one man said.

The house belonged to the town's notary public, Wilton Hatire, who had recently signed the documents for the Principlist Party's leading man, Windsor Gutros, allowing the party to hold the biggest fundraiser in Dormier without limitations to funding and endorsements. This was a blow to the Ethicginian Party, who had been slowly losing their campaign funds by an unknown source—from within their party or not, they could not locate the thief.

Lash Gorge Stratus stood up and turned around looking at the blazing house—the violent fire reflected in his eyes as he yawned and scratched his elbow. He kicked over a small statue which was in the front yard and spat.

The three cohorts laughed and shouted, telling their boss to join them in their efforts.

Let me enjoy the pleasure of watching, Lash Gorge Stratus said. Next time, I will be the first to set the fire.

Who is next? one of the men asked.

How about Judge Diandre Loft? Lash Gorge Stratus said.

The three men shouted louder, shooting their guns into the burning fire.

After Cirrus Stratus left the note for Vienna, he was kidnapped by Lash Gorge Stratus on his way back home. He had stopped to urinate in an alley when two of Lash Gorge Stratus's men came up from behind—this was while Cirrus Stratus's father and a few of his henchmen were torching Wilton the Notary's house. Cirrus Stratus felt their shadows creeping up behind him and he turned around in a rush, trying to urinate onto the two men. They jumped back instinctively, allowing Cirrus Stratus to throw punches in an effort to escape. He was able to hit one man in the face—causing him to fall back to the ground, but the other man grabbed hold of his other arm and twisted it back—pushing his body against the wall. The man slammed Cirrus Stratus repeatedly until his body went limp. The man let go and Cirrus Stratus fell to the ground but he still wasn't ready to give up.

While on the ground, Cirrus Stratus kicked him between the legs, and as he bent over in agony, Cirrus Stratus kicked him in the face. As that man went down, the other man got up. Cirrus Stratus was able to stand, too, but he couldn't swing his arms to punch—his shoulders were too sore for any movement after being slammed against the wall several times. The man choked Cirrus Stratus until he fell to his knees and then punched him until he fell to the ground.

When Cirrus Stratus became conscious, he felt the soreness in his ribs and shoulder. His head was ringing. His hands were tied behind his back, and he was blindfolded. He heard voices.

I'm very disappointed, he heard a voice say.

It was his father.

Son, Lash Gorge Stratus said. I'm very disappointed in you.

Cirrus Stratus couldn't recognize his voice—it had been too long since he had heard his father speak, and his father's voice had changed quite a bit since then. It had become much hoarser, deeper, more bitter.

What am I to do with you? the father said.

Kill him, answered one of Lash Gorge Stratus's men.

Then there was shouting—agreeing that they should kill Lash Gorge Stratus's son.

Lash Gorge Stratus put up his hand and there was silence. He walked up to his son and ran his hand down his hair. Cirrus Stratus moved his head to the side but his father slapped him and straightened his head. He pinched his cheeks and tugged on his earlobes.

Cirrus Stratus spat on his father's face. Lash Gorge Stratus slapped his son and wiped the spit off of his own cheek.

You have your mother's temper, the father said. Sometimes that's good. Sometimes it will get you in trouble. You should try to be more like your father.

My father is nothing more than squirrel urine, Cirrus Stratus said. He couldn't make it on his own so he traded his soul for a thousand souls.

Lash Gorge Stratus paced back and forth in front of his son. The men behind him laughed at his son's response. Lash Gorge Stratus put up his hand and the men stopped laughing. He told them to leave, and only Cirrus Stratus and his father remained in the room.

Your father doesn't trade, Lash Gorge Stratus said. He takes.

My apologies, Cirrus Stratus said. So then he is just dog excrement. Did you know that there was a time when my father would cry as the sun rose in the morning at the sight of its beauty.

Cirrus Stratus started to laugh.

He never saw me looking at him, Cirrus Stratus said. It was so embarrassing.

Lash Gorge Stratus slapped his son again but Cirrus Stratus laughed louder, and with each slap, his laughter increased.

He is such a timid frail little man, Cirrus Stratus said. I've seen stronger fleas.

He was laughing so hard he fell down on his back—tears coming down from his blindfolded eyes.

Lash Gorge Stratus dragged his son away from the wall and stood him up, and as Cirrus Stratus continued to laugh, the father closed his fists and started to beat his son until he fell back to the floor. His blindfold came off and Cirrus Stratus blinked repeatedly until he could focus. He saw his father and started to laugh again. He rolled around, back and forth and laughed until he was out of breath.

Look at you, Cirrus Stratus said. Look at you and your tiny little head.

Lash Gorge picked up his son and held him in the air and screamed—he threw Cirrus Stratus across the room. He watched his son roll until he hit the other side of the wall. Cirrus Stratus's eyes were closed—there was no laughter—

just blood and faint breathing. He was unconscious again for the second time that day.

His father dragged him to the corner of the room and left, mumbling to himself as he rubbed his sore knuckles.

Cirrus

Stratus had been stealing money from the Ethicginian Party. He would sneak into their main headquarters and break into the vault, slowly taking their money and keeping it safely hidden in a hole he dug just next to his hut. He didn't tell his mother because he knew she wouldn't allow it so he kept it in his dirt bank, saving up bit by bit, to help ensure a better future for his mother and himself. He hadn't spent any of it, though at times he wanted to—urges to buy gifts for his mother and Vienna. Instead, he just stole gifts for them.

Cirrus Stratus felt the barrel against his head—he recognized the smell of stale gunpowder. He showed no fear as he approached the proximity of death.

You have two choices, Lash Gorge Stratus said.

Cirrus Stratus kept his eyes open and looked directly at the cement wall in front of him. He was surrounded by dirt and the smell of decay of previous executions—whether dogs or humans, he couldn't tell. He tilted his head against the barrel. Lash Gorge Stratus pressed the revolver back against his head.

Leave, Lash Gorge Stratus said. On behalf of the Ethicginian Party, I hereby exile you for theft and betrayal.

Cirrus Stratus cracked his knuckles.

Or you die. And your mother dies.

Cirrus Stratus sighed and closed his eyes, picturing his mother, sitting at the table in the hut, sewing a sari. There's a cup of tea next to her threads, and she is humming and singing as she sews.

Your decision, Lash Gorge Stratus said.

Exile, Cirrus Stratus said.

You leave tonight, the father said. By boat—my men will take you to make sure the agreement is fulfilled.

Agreement, Cirrus Stratus laughed.

This is all your doing, Lash Gorge Stratus said. You've brought this upon yourself—betraying your own father.

My father had gentle eyes, Cirrus Stratus said.

I fed you, Lash Gorge Stratus said. I helped you fly your first kite.

You didn't, Cirrus Stratus said. My father was the one who showed me love.

You are Cirrus Stratus, the father said. You carry my last name.

I am Cirrus Stratus, the son said. You carry *my* last name.

Lash Gorge Stratus hit his son on the back of his head with the butt of the revolver, knocking him out. He put him in a large hay sack and dragged him back inside the headquarters and told his men to get ready to take a trip— to send his son into exile.

Vienna walked down the streets of the untouchables, going from hut to hut asking if anyone knew of Cirrus Stratus. Although some knew about him, they didn't say so in fear of getting into some kind of trouble with either Lash Gorge Stratus or his son, who had a reputation of brutality and violence. The others, who did not know of Cirrus Stratus, kept pointing down the street to ask someone else, and Vienna continued to do so.

She came to Alcee's place and Alcee was sitting at the table with a cup of tea. Her face was bruised and her hair was mangled—her clothes were torn, showing scrapes on her elbows and legs. She heard Vienna knocking on the wall and grabbed a lead pipe. She remained quiet.

Excuse me, Vienna said. I'm looking for someone and I was wondering if you could help me.

Alcee didn't say anything. She held the lead pipe with two hands cocked behind her head.

Cirrus Stratus, Vienna said. I'm looking for someone named Cirrus Stratus. He left a note for me.

The softness of Vienna's voice didn't ease any tension for Alcee—keeping the pipe cocked, she asked who was at the door.

My name is Vienna, she said. An untouchable.

Alcee lowered the pipe and kept it by her side. She told Vienna to come in.

Do you know Cirrus Stratus? Vienna asked.

He is my son, Alcee said.

Where is he?

I was hoping you would know, Alcee said. I haven't seen him in three days. I keep waiting to see his body dragged through the streets.

Vienna noticed Alcee's bruises and red eyes.

I have mango juice, Alcee said.

She poured the juice from a half broken pitcher into two tin cups and handed one to Vienna.

Do you need medical attention? Vienna asked. I know someone who could take a look at your cuts.

As Alcee took a sip of her juice, she looked at the top of her hand, grimacing as she looked at the five long cuts stemming from each knuckle.

No need, Alcee said. They will heal. But the loss of my son—I don't know if that can heal.

Vienna looked around the room and saw a broken glass swan in the corner of the room, where Cirrus Stratus slept.

Pretty, Vienna said.

Alcee followed Vienna's eyes to the corner of the room. She walked over and picked it up, holding it up to the hanging lantern. A part of its body had broken off, but Alcee looked through the back of the curved neck, through the bowed head, seeing a distorted Vienna. She handed the swan over to Vienna.

I have something like this, Vienna said.

Of course you do, Alcee said.

I didn't mean it like that, Vienna said. My apologies.

I didn't either, Alcee said. That was probably his seventh attempt of making that for you.

Vienna's eyes widened. She coughed and cleared her throat.

Did he make this? Vienna wondered.

For you, Alcee said.

Alcee sat down at the table, her palms wrapped around her cup of juice like as if it was keeping her hands warm.

He loves to create things out of glass, Alcee said. He has gotten a lot better, too.

She laughed.

His first attempt was supposed to be a flower of some sort but he could never get it right.

Alcee motioned to Vienna to sit.

I woke up one morning to the sound of glass crashing against the ground, Alcee said. He was practically in tears. But he kept working on it, and he had gotten better and better.

Why did he make these for me? asked Vienna.

My dear, Alcee said. For love.

How can he love me? Vienna said. We have never met. I have never spoken a word to him.

Alcee smiled.

Yes, she said. A silent love can be as strong as any other kind of love.

Vienna played with the glass swan—twirling it around and holding it up to the lantern, rubbing her fingers along its neck.

Even broken, Vienna said, it's powerful.

Vienna showed Alcee the note written by Cirrus Stratus.

He gave me two dead horses, she said. I don't know what to think.

His intentions are well meant, Alcee said, shaking her head. But his decisions and choices still need work.

I was frightened at first, Vienna said. I thought he was crazy.

He is crazy, Alcee said. And gone. I don't know where he is or if he's alive.

Vienna offered to help Alcee in finding Cirrus Stratus.

I would like to see the man who killed beauty for love, Vienna said.

Lash Gorge Stratus sat on the steps leading up to the headquarters of the Ethicginian Party. He held a rose in his hand, tracing his fingers along each petal, staring into the dirt before him. He was in a daze, with glossy eyes and tilted head. He heard a familiar voice, breaking his hypnotic state.

Where is Cirrus? Alcee asked.

Lash Gorge Stratus stood up and held out the rose for Alcee. She didn't make any motion to take the flower.

You look torn, Lash Gorge Stratus said. The streets are scraping your skin.

This is you and your men's doing, Alcee said.

I would never, he said.

What did you do with my son? Alcee demanded.

Come back to me, Lash Gorge Stratus said.

Alcee picked up a broken brick from the ground.

I am a widow, Alcee said.

He is gone, Lash Gorge Stratus said, lighting a cigar and blowing rings of smoke toward Alcee. You used to find this charming, he continued.

Where is he? Alcee asked again.

When Lash Gorge Stratus told Alcee about how he exiled him to an island, she threw the brick at him and hit him repeatedly on the body and face. Lash Gorge Stratus fell to the ground, still holding the cigar in his hand. He took a puff and laughed.

Be careful my dear, Lash Gorge Stratus said. Or you'll find yourself as not only a widow but a mother of the deceased.

Alcee kicked the cigar out of his hand.

You will be dead, she said.

After you, Lash Gorge Stratus said.

Still on the ground, he shouted and three men walked outside from the headquarters.

It takes you three men, Alcee said.

You should run, Lash Gorge Stratus said. I want to see you run.

Alcee stayed and watched the three men walk toward her. They asked Lash Gorge Stratus what they should do with Alcee.

Ask her, he said.

I'm not leaving until you tell me the location of this island.

Lash Gorge Stratus nodded his head at the three men.

Well, stay then, he said.

The three men grabbed Alcee but she fought back, swinging her arms and grunting. One man fell to the ground, yelping in pain. Lash Gorge Stratus laughed. Alcee turned around to fend off one of the other men, but couldn't act swiftly enough. She saw Lash Gorge Stratus's half-lit cigar before her eyes closed.

Vienna,

both out of her own curiosity and to help Alcee, had been asking the townspeople if they knew Cirrus Stratus or his whereabouts. Almost everyone was kind and responsive to her—her elegance and sweet voice had that effect on anyone around her.

Even the mosquitoes stop sucking blood just to hear your tongue, one old man said.

His name was Oncle Metia—he was Dormier's most prominent and well respected liar. He never lied to hurt anyone or to steal or cheat. He always lied to benefit the one who needed it the most. Vienna was well aware of this as she approached him.

My dear, she said. For once, speak the truth.

Look, Oncle Metia said.

He pointed to a mosquito that was hovering in the air, just next to Vienna's chin.

Why doesn't it suck your blood? he asked.

He coughed and ran his hand through the few strands of hair he had left.

It's because it knows better not to ruin beauty, he said. But me. It knows there is no beauty here and will needle me as soon as you go.

He laughed.

Please don't go away, Oncle Metia said. Please stay until the mosquito tires and drops to the ground to find Icarus and his melted wings.

Vienna smiled.

For a liar, she said, you have more charm than any truthful person I know. I should be careful.

As well you should, Oncle Metia said.

He lit a cigarette and coughed.

Never trust a man who is afraid of mosquitoes, he said.

He pushed down on his cane as he sat down in his wooden rocking chair. They were out on the porch of Oncle Metia's house—it was well away from the core of the town as he liked to keep alone and away from the city noise. He always welcomed visitors.

Now, Oncle Metia said. Who is it again? Who is the fellow blessed to have you in search of him?

Vienna sat down on the stoops leading up to his porch.

Cirrus Stratus, she said.

Ah yes, he said. Cirrus Stratus the Untouchable.

Vienna looked up at the lowering sun and closed her eyes. Oncle Metia looked at her face, her neck, and her lips.

So why would such beauty be in search of the dirt of an untouchable?

I am also an untouchable, Vienna said.

She kept her eyes closed.

Yes, he said. Yes, you are untouchable.

He gave me a most awkward and horrifying gift, Vienna said. I would just like to thank him and ask him about such a present.

You are looking for someone who does not exist, Oncle Metia said. You are looking for dead blood.

What do you know? Vienna asked. Is he dead? How do you know this?

She opened her eyes and looked at Oncle Metia's papery hands.

He is not here anymore, Oncle Metia said.

For a liar, you do seem to know a lot.

I have never told a lie, Oncle Metia said.

Where is he?

And what would you do if I told you? he said.

I will go find him, Vienna said. I will help him if he needs help. His mother worries for him.

Alcee, Oncle Metia said, smiling and coughing. Stay close to her. The world can learn much from the way she looks upon the sun and the city.

I'm trying my best to help her, Vienna said.

Find him, Oncle Metia said.

Tell me, she said.

There is this land, he said. Directly west from the coast, directly west from where we sit. It has no name. It has a belonging.

Vienna tilted her head and let the sun shine down on one side of her face.

It has a bloodied past, Oncle Metia said. It has the future of love.

Vienna thanked him and offered him a batch of aloe leaves. Oncle Metia rubbed his fingertips across them.

These are too soft for me, he said. I'm afraid my skin has hardened too much for any gentle touch.

I will be back, Vienna said. To repay you for your help.

Your visit was all I needed, Oncle Metia said. It was how I remembered it.

Vienna opened her mouth to question the meaning of Oncle Metia's statement but she kept it to herself and walked away.

Cirrus

Stratus woke up to see his own ghost standing in front of him, holding a rake.

You are my ghost, Cirrus Stratus said.

I am Cirrus Stratus the Ghost, the figure answered.

Where am I? Cirrus Stratus asked.

Cirrus Stratus the Ghost lifted his rake toward the sun and pushed it down into the sand. Cirrus Stratus noticed the cuts and bruises on his own arms and legs.

I am naked, Cirrus Stratus observed.

You are here, Cirrus Stratus the Ghost said.

Where? Cirrus Stratus said.

You are Cirrus Stratus the Exile.

Am I dead? Cirrus Stratus asked.

I am dead, Cirrus Stratus the Ghost answered.

Cirrus Stratus, grimacing and grunting, stood up and looked around and saw half cut palm trees made to look like wooden spikes. The tops lay in the sand, brown and withered.

Am I the only one here? Cirrus Stratus said.

I am here, Cirrus Stratus the Ghost replied.

Cirrus Stratus pulled two palm leaves off from one of the fallen branches and wrapped them around his waist. He started to shiver.

Come, Cirrus Stratus the Ghost said.

Cirrus Stratus followed his own ghost and they walked through the half cut trees, sharpened to look like teeth. He saw skulls and bones. He smelled the decay of flesh.

Is this Hell? Cirrus Stratus said.

Look, Cirrus Stratus the Ghost replied, pointing to one of the skulls.

There were mosquitoes hovering around its forehead.

Even the mosquitoes are tortured here, Cirrus Stratus the Ghost went on. The sun here does not soothe and warm.

He tapped his rake against the back of Cirrus Stratus's head.

Follow, he said.

They walked through the pathway of haunted trees— Cirrus Stratus the Ghost walked easily and without hesitation, but Cirrus Stratus kept being whipped and stung by the thin branches leaning over into the pathway. His body became covered in thin slashes of red—his head did, too. The land started to elevate, and it became harder and harder for Cirrus Stratus to walk as they ventured up a steep climb. Cirrus Stratus the Ghost appeared to be floating to Cirrus Stratus.

Are you walking? Cirrus Stratus wondered.

I am, Cirrus Stratus the Ghost said. We are almost to the clouds.

Feels like it, Cirrus Stratus said.

They reached the end of the climb. There was a horizon— the sun was muffled between the gray of the clouds. Cirrus Stratus felt dizzy and lost. Cirrus Stratus the Ghost took his hand and guided him to the edge of the cliff.

Look down, Cirrus Stratus the Ghost said.

Cirrus Stratus looked down and saw rows and rows of ditches—he could see people in each ditch. Some stood, some sat. Some were working hard, digging with shovels and rakes. Others were crying or rubbing the sweat off their bodies.

What is this? Cirrus Stratus asked.

This is mud and dirt and soil, Cirrus Stratus the Ghost said. They toil.

For what?

For their punishments, he said. They will dig until there is more to dig. They will dig dig dig. You will, too.

Why am I being punished? Cirrus Stratus said.

For living, Cirrus Stratus the Ghost said. And for living, you made me a ghost. I was fine where I was, but you brought me here, and now I will make you dig.

But what if I don't dig? Cirrus Stratus said.

You will become nothing but a skull, Cirrus Stratus the Ghost said.

He smiled and looked around the world, tapping his rake against the barren ground. Beyond the land, there was a dark ocean—the white foamed waves looked like teeth. A sudden wind made Cirrus Stratus realize that he was almost naked.

Come, Cirrus Stratus the Ghost said. Let's go meet your new friends.

They walked back down the path, the branches still whipping Cirrus Stratus, making him look like a tiger with stripes of skin and blood. They circled downwards, around and around—it was a different path from the one they followed on the way up. The smell of soil became stronger; the shrieks and shouts of pain became louder.

What have I done to deserve this? Cirrus Stratus said. Am I dead?

You are in between, Cirrus Stratus the Ghost said.

Is there a way to go back? Cirrus Stratus asked.

Cirrus Stratus the Ghost nodded.

Cirrus Stratus asked how he could go back to Dormier.

I will show you, Cirrus Stratus the Ghost said. Just listen and follow along. I surely don't want to be here, either.

Cirrus Stratus followed his own ghost down the path, to the ditches, where the scorned civilians toiled. There was shouting and yelps of pain—they were letting it be known to whoever would listen that they could no longer stand the burdens of their punishments. Cirrus Stratus the Ghost led Cirrus Stratus to a man who had no teeth—only a tongue kept a place in his mouth. His eyes were sunken in, and Cirrus Stratus could barely see them as his forehead and cheeks almost completely hid them. His bones were bulging out, and his skin wrapped tightly around them—over time, it stretched thinner and thinner to the point that one poke of the finger could pierce through.

What did he do? Cirrus Stratus wondered.

Ask him, Cirrus Stratus the Ghost said.

When he asked the hollow man, the punished stuck out his tongue, screamed and ran his fingers down his face, scratching and leaving red marks. Cirrus Stratus backed away and looked at his own ghost, who shrugged his shoulders as he twirled the rake in his hand.

Let me tell you instead, Cirrus Stratus the Ghost said. This man was a large, portly fellow who loved his veal and wine. He was a sculptor and had a good family life, but one day he found his wife in bed with a circus ringmaster.

Cirrus Stratus looked at the man, who had fallen to his knees, scraping the dirt with his wiry fingers, mumbling and crying.

With two hits of his chisel, both the wife and the circus conductor were dead, Cirrus Stratus the Ghost explained. He didn't even realize what he was doing and when he came back to reality, he had made marble statues of the two as he had seen them in bed. After one last thought, he killed himself with the same chisel.

Passion, Cirrus Stratus understood.

And stupidity, Cirrus Stratus the Ghost said. The circus conductor was just taking care of the wife because she had fallen ill and this man had been away for four months working on sculpting the sea.

The man tried to stand up but he fell backwards instead, his legs breaking into pieces. Cirrus Stratus the Ghost picked up the broken bones and handed them to him.

If you look at the statues, Cirrus Stratus said, you will see that the circus conductor is holding a thermometer and a mug, and the wife has her mouth open as if she's about to cough.

Cirrus Stratus looked around. He pointed.

And what about her, he said.

Cirrus Stratus the Ghost looked at the lady. She wore a shredded pink dress, and her hair was covered with twigs and mud. She was bent over, trying to pick out all of the dead worms from the barren earth.

She killed her father, Cirrus Stratus the Ghost said.

Why? Cirrus Stratus asked. I want to kill my own, too.

For no reason, Cirrus Stratus the Ghost said. She just woke up one morning and walked over to her parents' house, and filled her father's mouth with sand until his body stopped working.

So what am I to do? Cirrus Stratus said. Do I toil like them? Why am I here? I've killed no one. I've done nothing wrong.

All you've done is wrong, his ghost said. Apart from your love for your mother, your life is a nuisance.

So I am punished, Cirrus Stratus said.

So you are saved, Cirrus Stratus the Ghost said.

Alcee was hanging upside down from the branch of a banyan, blindfolded. She swung side to side, breathing in through her nostrils and exhaling through her mouth. With leaves caught in her hair, she started to sing.

Lash Gorge Stratus stood before her and listened. He closed his eyes and deeply breathed in. He saw his child on his knee. He saw his wife in the library room. He saw his father making a kite. He saw himself at dinner parties shaking hands with his friends and laughing, while holding a glass of red wine. He saw the river. Lash Gorge Stratus opened his eyes. Alcee continued to sing in a soft voice, carried away by the wind and the flying leaves. She stopped singing.

You're here, Alcee said.

I miss your songs, Lash Gorge Stratus said. Sing.

I only sing for the ones I love, Alcee said.

Lash Gorge Stratus picked up a dead branch—thin and curvy, with a few brown cracking leaves. He waved it through the air until the branch broke in half. He started to sing. It was a song he sang to Alcee while she was giving birth to Cirrus Stratus.

You were Leaus Perdu III once, Alcee said.

Lash Gorge Stratus continued to sing, running the dead branch against Alcee's upside down body.

You will never be the man you were then, Alcee said. You are now a disgrace.

Lash Gorge Stratus sang louder, keeping his eyes closed.

Your teeth are no longer pristine, she said. You no longer have a son.

Lash Gorge Stratus finished his song and opened his eyes and smiled. The sun came through the branches of the banyan—a bluebird perched itself next to Alcee, tilting its head.

You no longer have a son either, Lash Gorge Stratus said. Stay put.

He whistled while walking away—twirling the dead branch in the air.

Alcee turned her head toward the bluebird and whistled to it. The bird whistled back, in response, and Alcee pulled herself up—her stomach muscles, ripped and defined, were working to their utmost ability. She was able to sit upright on the branch, and she rubbed the rope tied around her wrists against the bark until the threads loosened. Still blindfolded, she lifted her head and let the divided sun streak upon her face. She untied her hands but she kept the blindfold on and sat there with the bluebird.

Vienna sat on the banks of the River Of Blue, running her fingers through the dirt. The river shone under the sun, making it look like a window—at certain spots, it was clear enough for Vienna to see the bed of the river and the fish hovering close alongside it. The note that Cirrus Stratus wrote to her was by her side, neatly folded. She still didn't know what to think of him or the note. She was confused. Two dead horses as a gift of love didn't make sense to her; however, her curiosity about the true meaning behind these actions kept her searching for Cirrus Stratus. She felt for his mother, too—she had taken an immediate liking to Alcee, upon their first visit.

She heard the crunching of leaves and smelled a familiar cologne—she spoke without turning around.

You're following me, Vienna said. Must I be spied upon?

Forgive me, my dear, Alejo said. I owe you an apology.

He put his hand on Vienna's shoulder, and she moved her body to the side.

Please, she said.

I understand, he said. I am grieved by your dislike for my presence but I understand.

Alejo walked past Vienna and walked to the banks of the river. He looked around and breathed in deeply. He closed his eyes and turned around, facing Vienna, and opened his eyes. He smiled.

Our last rendezvous was not the way I would have wanted it, Alejo said. I apologize for my antics—it was not my best side.

Vienna stared into the clumps of mud building up on the side of The River Of Blue. The river was quiet. The world was quiet. She didn't want to hear a sound—she just wanted to sit and stare into the water.

I would like to redeem myself, Alejo said.

Vienna didn't hear him, grazing her fingers through the dirt. She picked up broken twigs and fallen leaves and dropped them, repeatedly, forming some kind of rhythm. Alejo lifted Vienna's chin to get her attention, breaking her reverie.

I have two new horses, Alejo said. They are for you.

Please, Vienna said. No more gifts. I appreciate your offers, but I'm afraid I can no longer accept these presents. It isn't right on my part because there is no future for us.

Alejo sighed and stared through the trees on the other side of The River of Blue. His face scrunched up, becoming red—his eyes narrowed, tilted eyebrows.

You are in no position to decline my gifts, he said.

His voice was low and stern, barely making it through his gritted teeth. Vienna was surprised by his response but remained outwardly calm. She opened her mouth to speak but stopped herself. She waited for the silence between them to settle before she spoke.

You are too right, she said. I am in no position. I am an untouchable. This could never work. Please accept my humble apologies but I must remain within my own boundaries.

Alejo laughed—he cackled, lifting his face up toward the sky like a howling wolf. He kicked the dirt around him.

He started to pick up the dirt, cupping it in his hands, then throwing it in every direction. The branches and bushes shook as the wildlife—ranging from birds to anteaters—ran away, afraid. Vienna remained sitting on the ground as pieces of dirt hit her in the face and body. She closed her eyes and tilted her head to the side as Alejo threw bigger chunks of dirt.

You will regret this, Alejo said.

His fists were clenched—his eyes were red. Vienna remained in her meditative state with her legs crossed and her eyes closed. She breathed in and out in rhythm until finally she smiled and opened her eyes. Alejo continued to circle her.

I come from the streets, Vienna said. I have seen untouchables act with more grace and maturity than you.

Alejo rushed toward her, screaming, but Vienna remained still and continued to smile. He stopped right before her, almost falling over her.

You are nothing but a brat, she said.

Alejo lowered his body until his face was directly in front of Vienna's dirt covered head—he stared into her eyes and screamed. Vienna didn't move but looked directly into the back of Alejo's mouth.

Amazing, Vienna said. Even the untouchables have cleaner teeth than your yellow stained mouth.

Alejo raised his hand to strike her with his open palm.

You are nothing but brothel-born filth, Alejo said. You will die in the sweat of your mother while she opens her legs for two coins.

He swung his arm, just grazing the tip of Vienna's nose. She had yet to move or flinch. The sun shone down on her face through the wind rattled leaves, and kept her skin warm, making her feel protected by a shield of light.

Alas, Vienna said. You have covered my life well—in just a few sentences.

She laughed, making Alejo run his hands through his hair, pulling it and clenching it.

And what have you done but fall in love with a whore's daughter? she said.

Vienna brushed the dirt off her face and body and stood up, facing Alejo.

Take heed of my threats, little girl, Alejo said. Or you will find yourself in danger. If not you, then the ones around you.

It is hard to take threats, my dear, Vienna said, from a man who cannot keep his own horses.

Vienna walked away, not taking the natural path back to the city, but through the untouched foliage, tied in knots and mazes. Alejo remained behind staring into his own hands. He whispered to himself, I am sorry, and then he lifted his head and shouted as Vienna was no longer visible.

You will regret this, he said. You will feel blood.

Cirrus

Stratus shoveled horse manure. He dug into a massive mound of it and tossed it over his shoulder, forming another pile. This was his punishment—shoveling a never-ending tower of horse manure. He had to stop from time to time to vomit from the stench but if he waited too long to get back to shoveling, the mound would get bigger and bigger until he couldn't see its ending in the sky. If, even then, he still didn't begin to shovel again, Cirrus Stratus the Ghost would appear and start throwing pieces of manure at Cirrus Stratus until he started to dig again.

He was taking a break after vomiting—too long of a break—and Cirrus Stratus the Ghost appeared, throwing manure at him.

Quit it, Cirrus Stratus said.

Get to digging, Cirrus Stratus the Ghost said.

He threw another chunk at him and laughed—in his other hand, he held a glass of iced tea. Cirrus Stratus asked for a sip while picking up the shovel.

You don't deserve a drink, Cirrus Stratus the Ghost said. Once you're halfway done, you can get a sip.

You've gotten meaner, Cirrus Stratus said.

I am your ghost, Cirrus Stratus the Ghost replied.

Cirrus Stratus spat and stopped himself from using his forearm to wipe the sweat off his face. He spat again. The mound continued to get bigger.

This is pointless, he said. When I killed those two horses, I had a point.

For love, Cirrus Stratus the Ghost said.

For love, Cirrus Stratus said. Have you seen her?

I am your ghost, Cirrus Stratus the Ghost said.

Cirrus Stratus's eyes became large and glassy. They were full of energy as he thought about Vienna.

She reminds me of the mornings, he said. She reminds me of everything that makes me happy.

So you killed some horses, Cirrus Stratus the Ghost said. It's not just that. You're a thief, a robber, you're a troublemaker. Your life is no good.

But you don't understand, ghost, Cirrus Stratus said.

He twirled the shovel like it was a baton, smiling. He felt dizzy.

Have you ever been in love?

A distant cry could be heard, coming from a punished one. Both Cirrus Stratus and his ghost looked around and saw an emaciated figure trying to set himself on fire but the wind kept on blowing out the flame.

I'm not allowed to be, Cirrus Stratus the Ghost said.

He sipped his iced tea.

It wasn't out of anger or hate, Cirrus Stratus said. I did it for love.

Some love, Cirrus Stratus the Ghost said. I would think a bouquet of flowers would have been a bit better, less violent.

But that is all I know, Cirrus Stratus said.

He looked up at the sun, pointing the shovel toward it. The pile of manure became bigger and bigger, but Cirrus Stratus didn't care. Thinking about Vienna had led him to not care about anything else.

Let me out of here, Cirrus Stratus said. And I'll make things right.

I know your mind, Cirrus Stratus the Ghost said. You still have vengeance there. You are still no good.

How could I not have anger? Cirrus Stratus asked. I don't know if my mother is alive anymore. My father is evil itself, and he has no boundaries. Alejo and Vienna could be married now, for all the wrong reasons.

You are an untouchable, Cirrus Stratus the Ghost said.

I will always be an untouchable, Cirrus Stratus said.

He spat and scratched his chin with the handle of the shovel.

The streets are in my blood, he continued. There is nothing like it.

But you have been scorned and looked down upon, Cirrus Stratus the Ghost said. How could you want to be an untouchable?

Cirrus Stratus didn't answer him and started to shovel again. He was smiling as he dug into the mound of manure, taking in deep breaths and exhaling loudly. Cirrus Stratus the Ghost stood and watched as the distant cries of the man who was trying to set himself on fire continued to make its way to their ears. Cirrus Stratus started to sing and whistle. He was having fun. The sun was disappearing and a strong wind was coming in as well as dark clouds. It started to rain. Cirrus Stratus continued to sing and whistle, occasionally looking up at the sky to see the drops coming down on him.

This is how it gets done, Cirrus Stratus said. I had forgotten, but this is how it gets done. This is why I am an untouchable.

Cirrus Stratus the Ghost started to whistle along, realizing that Cirrus Stratus was making progress in the world between life and death—realizing that Cirrus Stratus has recognized the importance of being an untouchable.

You are working hard now, Cirrus Stratus the Ghost said.

My mother taught me how to work hard, Cirrus Stratus said. My mother works like no other, with love and gratitude.

With delight, Cirrus Stratus the Ghost said.

Cirrus Stratus, who was of small stature, began to show muscles. His biceps became larger, tighter, and his lower back, which was hurting before, was now becoming stronger and sturdier. His thigh muscles bulged with each dig, and his shoulders worked in rhythm with the rest of his body. He was working at such a fast rate, the mound was lessening. Cirrus Stratus the Ghost was impressed.

You seem to be finding a good pace, the ghost said. You seem to be in another world.

Well aren't we in another world? Cirrus Stratus said. Am I not alive? Am I not dead?

The mound was becoming closer and closer to the barren land, and though more manure came from the sky, it didn't make a difference to Cirrus Stratus as he worked in the rain and thunder. Cirrus Stratus the Ghost was hit by lightning strikes several times as he stood there, but he laughed every time he was struck, still taking sips from his never-ending iced tea.

Cirrus Stratus was able to work at a faster pace than the

clumps of manure falling from the sky. When there was nothing before him, he looked up at the clouds—-it was still raining and thundering. He was breathing hard, but he still managed to whistle between his huffs. He looked at Cirrus Stratus the Ghost, who was now lying down—a large chunk of clay was his pillow. His eyes were closed. Cirrus Stratus looked at the ground and saw one blade of grass growing. He knelt down and blew on it.

I'm done, Cirrus Stratus said. What should I do next?

Cirrus Stratus the Ghost didn't wake up. Cirrus Stratus poked him with the handle of the shovel but he didn't move. Cirrus Stratus stood and looked at him. He looked at the sky again, and then he looked all around, seeing what his fellow punished folk were doing in the stripped lands of neither his world nor the other.

I will wait then, Cirrus Stratus said.

He stood there in the rain and waited.

Lash Gorge Stratus stood at the edge of the cliff, looking over Dormier. A vulture walked around him in circles as he smoked a cigar and blew rings into the sky. It was morning—the ground was still wet with dew. He gazed into the town as it was beginning to wake up. The vulture looked at him one last time before flying away.

Lash Gorge Stratus bent down and picked up a newly handmade kite—he hadn't made one in 20 years, and the last time he had flown one was with his son.

Before we crumble, Lash Gorge Stratus said. No. Before I crumble.

He knew he had turned. He knew he had changed. He knew he was no good. He accepted that his life would lead to nowhere, but he would never let anyone know. He was driven by the machine he had created, in search of power. The idea of instilling fear in others was what made him go deeper and deeper into his own dark soul.

He backed away from the cliff and once he thought he was far enough, he started to run as fast as he could, letting the kite trail behind him. Right before he hit the edge of the cliff, the kite soared—fluttering back and forth with no rhythm in the morning winds. With one hand holding the kite, and the other hand holding his cigar, Lash Gorge Stratus maneuvered the kite with ease, as if he had been flying kites every day for 40 years.

This is all so infinite, Lash Gorge Stratus said.

He had acknowledged that he had started talking to himself more and more lately, and the more he talked to himself, the lonelier he became.

Without hesitation, he thought about Cirrus Stratus, Alcee, and his own father, Leaus Perdu II.

Oh father, Lash Gorge Stratus said. You were such a fool.

He puffed his cigar.

Oh father, if I could ever be like you.

A strong wind came in and the kite almost pulled Lash Gorge Stratus off the cliff.

I have forgotten how to cry, he said.

He put his cigar against the kite's string until it burned all the way through, letting the kite go whichever way the wind took it. It flew toward the sun. He thought back to when Leaus Perdu II would take him out to the cliff for lunch. His mother, Dimanche Fridatte Charon Perdu, would make biscuits and jelly, sausage and syrup every Sunday for the two, and they would take the carriage out to the trail and then walk to the cliff where they had a clear view of the city under the sun. They would talk all the way to the cliff, but when they reached their spot, the talking ceased, and it became more of a meditation for the two— quietly unwrapping the food while Leaus Perdu II puffed on a cigar, and Leaus Perdu III would become hypnotized by the sun.

When his father did talk it would be about family history, giving him life lessons. Lash Gorge Stratus remembered how his eyes lit up as he talked about their family's journey into the volcano, and how they made a living for themselves from nothing but the love for food and crafts.

We were what they called untouchables back then, he said. But everyone was untouchable back then. Never forget, son.

What's an untouchable? Leaus Perdu III asked.

Someone who knows life, Leaus Perdu II said. Someone who understands the true identity of humility.

Lash Gorge Stratus continued to watch the kite flutter toward the sun. He then shifted his glance to Dormier, and spotted the area where he and his family used to live.

You could sing, Lash Gorge Stratus said. You could sing the town into a trance.

Alejo went to the stable to look at the two new horses he had bought for Vienna—his gifts which were denied by her. He whispered to them and ran his hands along each of their necks. His eyes became red and the whispering turned into heavy breathing and grunting. He stopped petting them.

Vienna Vienna, Alejo said.

He shouted for his servant, Thuroon. He shouted his name again, his voice thundering around inside the stable, making the horses move about.

Vienna, Alejo said.

He punched one of the horses. He punched the other horse. They both snorted and grunted and shuffled about, showing unease and anxiety. He punched them again and shouted for his servant. He came in, running, and huffing.

Where were you? Alejo said. You are my servant. I've been waiting for you for too long.

Sorry, sir, Thuroon said. I was plowing the fields.

Plow, Alejo said. Go plow.

Sorry, sir, the servant said.

Go plow, Alejo repeated.

Thuroon turned around to go back to the fields. Alejo shouted again.

Thuroon, Alejo said. Turn around.

The servant stopped and faced Alejo.

Sir, he said.

Where is my rifle, Alejo said.

Sir, he said. It's in the library, sir, along with the rest of your collection.

Why are you still here? Bring it to me now.

Yes sir, Thuroon said.

He started to run toward the mansion. Alejo shouted his name again. Thuroon made a circular motion and started to go back to the stable. He leaned over, breathing hard.

Stand straight, Alejo said.

He stood straight and tried to quiet his breathing.

Sir, Thuroon said.

Bring me my rifle, Alejo said.

Yes sir, he said.

The servant waited to see if Alejo wanted anything else.

Why are you still here? Alejo said.

Thuroon ran back to the mansion, as he was trying to do before, to get Alejo's rifle. Alejo stared at the horses while the servant was away. He kept his hands by his sides, facing them. He looked at them with their red eyes, with red faces, with red skin. The horses lowered their heads, not looking Alejo in the eyes. The servant came back holding Alejo's rifle in one hand and a small box of bullets in the other. He was sweating and breathing hard.

Present yourself properly, Alejo said. And quiet down.

Thuroon tucked in his shirt and brushed off the dirt on his pants and boots. He wiped the sweat from his face using a handkerchief.

Load it, Alejo said.

Thuroon loaded the rifle and gave it to Alejo.

Stay here, Alejo said.

Thuroon was becoming nervous and started moving side to side. He did not like what was taking place but he was not in a position to let his feelings be known, for he feared losing his job. He had a family—a wife and two children—and they all worked, and if one of them were to lose their job, their living conditions would be in great danger. They would have to move to the streets. Thuroon was a kind man—a hard and loyal worker, and a good family man. Before working for Alejo, he cleaned the gutters of Dormier, and one day, while working on one of the gutters, Alejo hired Thuroon on the spot, as he had just fired his previous servant for eating his dinner at the table.

Sweet horses, Alejo said. Loving horses.

He aimed the rifle at one of the horses' heads. His hand shook and he took a deep breath, trying to keep the rifle steady. Thuroon closed his eyes—he thought about his children and wife. He wished he was back at home, at the dinner table, getting ready to eat curry and cauliflower. He didn't hear anything and opened his eyes, seeing Alejo still aiming the rifle at the head of one of the horses.

Servant, Alejo said.

Sir, Thuroon said.

Come here, Alejo said. Stand next to me.

Thuroon stood next to him. Alejo lowered his rifle, and Thuroon sighed. He wanted to express his relief to Alejo, but he kept silent. The horse's head remained lowered, refraining from looking at Alejo in the eyes or at the rifle.

Take it, Alejo said.

He pushed the rifle into Thuroon's body—he took the rifle and un-cocked it.

Keep it cocked, Alejo said. You will shoot these two beautiful horses.

Sir, Thuroon said.

You will shoot these two beautiful horses, Alejo said. Or you will be fired.

But sir, Thuroon protested.

Before he could finish his sentence, Alejo interrupted him.

Think about your family, he said. Do you want to go back to the gutter? Do you want to starve your family? Do you want to live on the streets?

No sir, Thuroon said.

He lifted the rifle and cocked it. He whispered.

Sorry, he said.

He thought of a prayer and closed his eyes. He took a deep breath and closed his eyes as hard as he could.

Alcee was back at the hut—the place had been ransacked while she was away, tied to the banyan by Lash Gorge Stratus. She started to clean her place and put her salvageable belongings back in their original spots to make it feel like home as much as possible.

She heard a soft voice coming from outside, calling her name, and she recognized it.

Come in, Vienna, Alcee said.

Vienna walked in, still holding Cirrus Stratus's note—it hadn't left her side since she had received it on that day he had killed two horses for her.

I miss him, Alcee said.

I've tried looking for you, Vienna said.

I've gathered that he has been sent away in exile, Alcee said, smiling. He is still alive—only Cirrus Stratus can cause so much chaos. We will find him. Or he will find us.

Vienna helped throw away the various broken pieces caused by the ransacking. When they were done, they sat at the table and Alcee poured a cup of mango juice for her.

This is delicious, Vienna said.

Cirrus Stratus can find the best mangoes in town, Alcee said. He has a secret spot—he won't tell me where he gets it from. I'm sure they are stolen.

He lives a rough life, doesn't he? Vienna wondered.

Alcee stood up and looked at a broken candle holder Cirrus Stratus had given to her.

Moving to the streets and becoming an untouchable has been tough for him, Alcee said. It's funny—he has always been good to me. He has always shown love for me. He is a wonderful son.

She picked up the candle holder.

But when it comes to other people, Alcee said, he can't find it in himself to respect them. Everything he does—the stealing and fighting, the constant troublemaking—he does it for me. He wants me to be happy, and he's trying his best to give me the life we had before moving to the streets.

Alcee turned toward Vienna and sat back down.

And now, she said. He does it for you, too.

Vienna raised her eyebrows.

But how can he love someone he doesn't know? We've never met.

Alcee tilted her head back and looked at the ceiling made of straw and clay.

Have you ever been in love? Alcee said.

Vienna shook her head.

For you, Alcee said, it must be tough, as you have so many suitors. It can be hard to tell if someone truly loves you or if you are just an untouchable prize.

What about your son? Vienna said. Do you think it's true?

Of course, Alcee said. Cirrus Stratus only acts with true intentions. He has never hidden anything—his emotions or thoughts. Perhaps, it is both his best quality and worst quality—it gets him in trouble most of the time.

She laughed.

He loves you, Alcee continued. Because he sees the world in you. He sees the softness in you—a softness he seeks because he has never felt anything other than the grit of the streets.

Vienna fiddled with her cup—Cirrus Stratus's note, neatly folded beside her. The wind started to pick up, making the rug door wave in the air, giving glimpses of the untouchable streets before them.

True, Alcee said. At first, he had a wealthy lifestyle, but that is easy to forget just after two weeks of being an untouchable. Working in the gutters, stealing, trying to stay warm—all of these things force him to live in the present.

You two are very close, Vienna said. I admire that. Despite the troubles you all have gone through—that he has gone through—the love you have for each other is unbending.

Perhaps the troubles have made us become closer, Alcee said. It could be a lot worse, perhaps. I know he's thinking that I'm worried about him.

We'll find him, Vienna said. I would like to tell him hello.

Sari had Alejo down on his knees. His hands were tied behind his back, covered in sweat. He was breathing hard, trying his best not to cry in front of his captor. He said he was sorry repeatedly, almost sounding like a chant. He kept his head down, facing the marble floor of his own bathroom, and he rocked his body back and forth. Sari held a whip made of twigs and vines. Her smile revealed her bright teeth, perhaps the whitest of all untouchables.

What do you do now, Mr. Alejo, she said.

Stop, Alejo said. Please.

Tell me, Sari said.

She spoke in a soft voice.

Tell me what you wanted to do to me when we were at the saloon, Mr. Alejo.

I'm sorry, he said. I will be more respectable.

I am a whore, Sari said. Or at least I *was* a whore. No need to be sorry.

You're a beautiful lady, Alejo said.

You're in a predicament, Sari said.

She raised the whip and lashed it onto the floor right next to him. Alejo flinched. He had a cut under his right eye, but it wasn't from his current situation. It happened at the saloon as Sari was trying to protect herself from a drunken Alejo, who was aggressively trying to get a kiss from her. She had gone to the saloon to see if she could find any information about Cirrus Stratus and his whereabouts. She saw former clients; scarred faces and red eyes, their looks had not changed since Sari was in the business of prostitution. Some were happy to see her, as she was considered the best in town during those days, while others looked the other way, hoping they weren't remembered. No one knew anything, and Sari believed them. As she was about to leave the saloon, she saw Alejo sitting alone at a table taking shots of whiskey. She did not know about his last encounter with Vienna so when she pulled a seat next to him, her intentions were to be cordial. Alejo, however, had other thoughts in mind.

Alejo lifted his head with much effort and glared at Sari with dark red eyes. He puffed his cigar and blew the smoke into her face.

Yes, Alejo said. The whore's whore.

Sari had ignored his comment, giving his drunken state the benefit of the doubt and proceeded to retrieve information.

Good sir, she said. Please tell me if you know of Cirrus Stratus's whereabouts.

Alejo looked around the room, and then up at the ceiling.

Probably dead, he said. He's probably dead by now.

Where would he be dead? Sari asked.

Exiled and dead, Alejo said. What disgust your daughter has caused me. She will have regrets, too, much like Cirrus Stratus.

Hearing this, Sari changed her manner and tone. The demeanor from her past life took control of her. She pulled the cigar out of his mouth and threw it on the floor, stepping on it.

Such threats will get you into trouble, Sari warned.

Alejo tried to stand up in anger but he couldn't balance himself and quickly sat back down so he wouldn't fall.

The town's finest gentleman, Sari said.

Alejo leaned over and tried to kiss Sari. She moved her head back. He tried to put his arm around her shoulder but she denied him.

For a whore, Alejo said, you are quite choosy, it seems. Perhaps we should refresh your memory of how to be one. Let's go upstairs.

Please, Sari said. You have no clue how to be with a woman or a whore. Or even my daughter.

Alejo slammed his fists onto the wooden table, causing it to splinter.

Where is Cirrus Stratus? Sari asked again.

If we go upstairs, Alejo said. I'll tell you.

Sari knew where this was leading, but she agreed, just in case Alejo was drunk enough to let her know about Cirrus Stratus. She followed him upstairs. A series of memories flashed through her mind with each step. They found a room, and Alejo started to take off his tie and unbuckle his belt.

First tell me, Sari said.

Imbecile, Alejo said, stumbling. As if I were to tell you. I'm not even here for your services.

He took off his belt and folded it in half, holding it like a whip.

I'm here to make your daughter regret, Alejo said.

He lifted his arm to lash Sari, but she moved out of the way, and in the same motion, she punched Alejo under the eye. Embarrassed and angry, Alejo left the room, stumbling and hitting the sides of the walls as he bled from the split skin under his eye. Sari waited a few moments before following him—she hitched a ride on the back of his carriage and rode it all the way back to his manor. There, she hid in the garden. She peeked through one of the windows and saw Alejo taking a shot of liquor. She made a whip out of the vines growing in the front of the house, tying twigs to it to give it some weight. Alejo took seven more shots before leaving the kitchen. He left the front door wide open, and Sari quietly walked inside without any trouble. She heard the shuffling of feet and followed the sound until she found him in the bathroom with marble flooring, trying to tend to his cut. Sari surprised him, kicking the back of his knees, making Alejo fall to the ground, leading to the predicament he was now in.

Just as Sari was about to use the whip again to scare Alejo, she smelled stale gunpowder and metal, and felt a small round object pressed against the back of her head. Thuroon stood behind her, holding Alejo's rifle. His hands shook, and his voice quivered.

Please, Thuroon said. Madame, please. Please kindly leave.

Where have you been? Alejo said. Tend to my cut after you end her.

Sari looked at Thuroon and noticed his gentle, watery eyes. The sound of his voice was soothing to her, and she could tell that he wasn't a killer. She dropped the whip and fixed her hair. Alejo tried to stand up but Sari pushed her foot on his back to keep him down.

End her, Alejo said.

Madame, Thuroon said. Please.

She smiled and walked out of the bathroom, leaving Thuroon with Alejo. She turned around before exiting the hallway, seeing Thuroon trying to help Alejo stand up while at the same time, being scolded for taking too long to save him, and for not killing Sari.

Thuroon was back at home. He sat at the dinner table alongside his wife, Medalia, and his son, Bhava, and daughter, Mary Maria. His children were 7 and 12 years old, Bhava being the older one. Their love for their parents and each other was all they had as they didn't go to school or have a life outside of their family and work. Medalia was a haberdasher and through her diligence and fine crafting, she had gradually made a name for herself with various vendors in Dormier. She divided her time with work and teaching her children school subjects, only sleeping four hours a night. Thuroon helped as much as he could but his time devoted to Alejo prohibited him from too much freedom.

Thuroon sat at the dinner table and looked around. He looked at his wife and sighed as the smell of lentils and curry filled the room. His children were setting the table, singing a song about chimney sweeping. Thuroon stood up to get the cups and fill them with water.

I'll get it daddy, Bhava said. Please, sit.

Thuroon patted him on the back and then gave both of his children a hug. He walked up to Medalia, who was writing a note, something work related. He kissed her cheek. She kissed him back.

Come, Thuroon said. Let's eat this fine scented dinner.

I'll be right there, Medalia said. Just didn't want to forget about making a set of buttons for the store down the road.

Bhava and Mary Maria shouted that it was time to eat—they had cooked this particular dinner together and were excited about how it looked. They wanted everyone to taste it before it went cold.

Thuroon and Medalia had met in the gutters—it was where they fell in love. Thuroon was working under the streets cleaning the pipes when he heard a shout for help not too far down. Medalia had fallen into the gutters while escaping bandits who wanted a plate of food she was carrying to her family's home. When Thuroon found her, he saw her standing, covered in dirt and sludge, with her arm raised above her, holding the plate.

Please, she said. Save the plate—it's for my grandmother. It's her birthday today, can you please take it to her?

Thuroon was speechless, as her beauty had immediately taken over him.

You have very pretty eyes, he said. Eyes that soften the world.

Please, Medalia said. I'm in no state of beauty. Look at me—I'm here in the gutters, covered in such mess.

Would you like to go up? Thuroon offered.

Do you think you can save this plate? Medalia asked.

I think, more than anything else, you have saved me.

Thuroon took out a pocket candle and lit it, and held it to her face.

Excuse my appearance, he said. But may we have dinner one night? I'm a horrible cook, but I will cook for you with such passion.

Medalia looked at Thuroon, taken aback. Her day was so unusual, and it was becoming odder and odder. The pipes were making noises. Thuroon wiped his hands on his pants and held them out.

Come, he said. Follow me. I will show you the way to the land above the sewers.

When they were above ground, Thuroon dusted off the dirt on his clothes, forming clouds of grit. He looked up and smiled, showing bright white teeth. Medalia was still holding the plate of food.

Looks like your grandmother will be able to have a good dinner, he said.

Thank you so much for your help, Medalia said.

Please, Thuroon said. I will cook for you.

Medalia looked into his eyes and fell into a dream. Thuroon brushed her hair aside.

I feel like you were supposed to fall into the sewer, he said. Gutter love.

Medalia couldn't stop looking into Thuroon's eyes. He kept smiling and looking back at her. He called her name a few times, until Medalia was out of her trance. She said yes to dinner and Thuroon told her where he lived. Two days later, she went over to his house, ate the worst cooking she ever had and fell in love with Thuroon.

Thuroon and his family sat at the dinner table. Medalia asked him about his day. He bowed his head for a brief moment and looked up. There were a few tears straying from his eyes.

I'm thinking about quitting, he said. I want to go back to the gutters, with your blessing.

Medalia finished her bite and looked at Thuroon the same way she had done when they first met.

You will always have my blessing, she said. It is your passion. Alejo is not a good man.

Thuroon kissed her on the forehead, thanking her. He stared at his food wondering how he could get away from Alejo.

As Cirrus

As Cirrus Stratus waited for his own ghost to wake up, he started to help those who were also punished and exiled to the unknown island that existed between life and death. There was a child sitting underneath a barren tree—withered branches, covered in dying leaves, thin and frail roots. The boy sat there, in rags—his back against the weak bark of the tree. Cirrus Stratus approached him to see if he needed any help.

Your name? Cirrus Stratus said.

I am Banya, he said.

His eyes had lost all signs of life—small and watery, lacking energy. Cirrus Stratus bent down on one knee.

I am Cirrus Stratus, he said. I've been sent here because of my own scorn and the scorn of others. I hope to return soon.

Banya looked up into the sky, scratching both of his knees. His hair had grown long, down to the middle of his back. In between the rags, Cirrus Stratus could see his ribs pressing hard against the inside of his skin.

I've been cursed to sit under this tree for eternity, Banya said. I've been sitting here, by my count, for about 5 years. I have a long way to go.

Cirrus Stratus asked him why he had been sent to the island.

I killed 10 men, Banya said. All at the same time.

Cirrus Stratus nodded and asked him why.

They beat my mother because she couldn't pay her bills. They were cowards. I shouldn't have killed them though. I should have just let them suffer.

How can such a young child kill so many people? Cirrus Stratus asked.

All I needed was a rake and a marble, Banya said. I have no regrets.

Your passion had gotten the best of you, Cirrus Stratus said. The same happened to me.

Banya looked up at Cirrus Stratus—first, at his chin, then his nose, then his eyes.

I have killed animals, Cirrus Stratus said. Stolen. Fought. I am a thug, a scoundrel. All because of passion.

Banya ran his hands along the dying roots, falling into a daze. Cirrus Stratus looked out into the barren fields and laughed.

Funny, he said. You killed. But you killed for the love of your mother. For protection. I think one day you'll see your mother again.

He sat down next to Banya and felt the dead land, pressing his palms against it. He sat alongside him for three days, both not saying a word to each other. They just sat there. Sometimes it rained. Sometimes the sun peeked through the gray, dead skies—but only for a bit. There were just glimpses of light. On the third day, Cirrus Stratus stood up and stretched. He patted Banya on the head and walked away.

See you, Banya said. My friend.

My friend, Cirrus Stratus said. See you.

Cirrus Stratus the Ghost was still sleeping so Cirrus Stratus continued to walk around to see if he could help anyone. He found a lady in a white dress made of silk, with holes in it, and its edges ragged. She had long black hair, shiny. Her skin was bronze. Her body was thin framed—her teeth bright white.

You are too pretty to be here, Cirrus Stratus said.

She spat.

Why are you here? Cirrus Stratus asked her.

The lady spat again. She held a rag and pitcher full of dark liquid. Cirrus Stratus introduced himself.

I am Gabriella Mariello, she said. I killed myself and woke up here.

There was a breeze—the first breeze Cirrus Stratus felt since shoveling the manure. He lifted his face toward the sky and closed his eyes. Gabriella's dress fluttered in the wind, making her look like a majestic ghost. Glimpses of her thighs exposed to the air, she stood still. Cirrus Stratus opened his eyes.

I'm beginning to like this place, he said.

It gets worse and worse for me, Gabriella said.

Your punishment? Cirrus Stratus asked.

She dipped the rag into the pitcher and got down on all fours.

I must polish the dirt, she said.

She took a handful of land and scrubbed it with the rag. She put the dirt back down, patted it, and picked up another bit of dirt and polished it. She continued to do so. Cirrus Stratus ripped off a piece of her rag and got down on his knees and proceeded to help her.

Perhaps, he said. We will bring this place back to life.

I hope that I will be dead by then, she said.

Why? Cirrus Stratus asked. Why do you want to be dead? Why did you kill yourself?

Gabriella spat and sighed. My life was no good. I lived on the streets, and I saw the worst of the worst—been through the worst of the worst. Why live? There was nothing to look forward to. I had no one.

I lived the same life, Cirrus Stratus said. I know your troubles. But now, we are here together.

Gabriella Mariello managed to smile. Cirrus Stratus stood up and started to whistle.

It's quite a day, he said.

He continued to whistle and Gabriella Mariello stood up and joined along. They stood there and whistled and hummed until the sky changed colors.

I will see you again, Cirrus Stratus said.

I wish you well, Gabriella Mariello said. Who knows.

Cirrus Stratus the Ghost was awake and lively. He was whistling and hopping around as Cirrus Stratus walked toward him.

Mighty good day, Cirrus Stratus the Ghost said.

Didn't think you'd ever awaken, Cirrus Stratus said.

You've been impressive, the ghost said. No one has ever fulfilled their punishment here. This quickly, too. I knew I had it in me.

May I go home? Cirrus Stratus asked.

Cirrus Stratus the Ghost shook his head.

Not yet, he said. There will be a time. But now is not the time.

I've lost all concept of time, Cirrus Stratus said.

He and his ghost looked around—all had disappeared. There was no one else—the punished were no longer there. It was just the two of them standing in the middle of a withering field, full of broken roots with no trees. Large birds were swirling above them. It was cold and the land was divided into rows—remnants of what used to be a place full of crops. Now there was nothing. Cirrus Stratus the Ghost smiled.

Make this place come alive, he said.

To satisfy his rage against Sari, Alejo didn't go straight for her, but instead to whom she loved the most. Vienna had been kidnapped. The news of her disappearance had quietly spread around the streets. The untouchables kept silent though—they were afraid to openly talk about it because they were worried that they would be kidnapped next. Everyone was silent. Sari was the only one crying out loud— she was the only one seeking answers for her daughter's disappearance and everyone she approached kept quiet, as if they did not know how to speak.

Vienna was tied at the wrists and legs, lying on a concrete floor in one of the backrooms of Lash Gorge Stratus's headquarters. The place was kept dim—the lights barely worked, and they hummed loudly. Mold covered the edges of each wall, from one wall to the other. Drips from a pipe came down from the ceiling forming puddles in various spots of the room. Vienna was intentionally not blindfolded. Lash Gorge Stratus wanted her to feel as uncomfortable as possible by her surroundings. However, Vienna was not scared. She had seen and been through too much for this experience to affect her. More than anything else, she felt at home. She missed her mother and hoped she was well but her worries didn't extend beyond that. She thought about Sari, and then Cirrus Stratus.

Who are you? she said. I would love to meet you.

Lash Gorge Stratus walked in. He had thinned quite a bit—his face, sickly looking and sunken. His eyes were dark red, showing a lack of rest and an abundance of liquor.

They revealed bitterness and scorn. He held a pistol in one hand and a cauliflower in the other. He stopped in front of Vienna, listening to the hum of the broken lights and the drips from the ceiling forming a puddle. He gave her the vegetable and pointed the pistol at her head.

You're beautiful, Lash Gorge Stratus said.

There was a time, Vienna said, when you were full of love and compassion.

Her words put him into a daze. He had memories. He thought about his son as a baby. He thought about his wife. There was a time when they were all together, happy. There was a time when life was full of kites, cooking, music, and love. He thought about the time when they went to the park inside the volcano and watched the swans gracefully floating in the lake that had formed on the day of his mother's death.

Those who were close to Lash Gorge Stratus at that time say he wasn't the same since the death of his mother. It didn't immediately trigger his transition from Leaus Perdu III to Lash Gorge Stratus, but it provided a hole in his soul that couldn't be filled with love anymore—only power and greed and fear. His father, who had a difficult time coping with his wife's passing, told his friends and relatives that his son had lost the love he had in his eyes after her death. If his mother was still alive, he would tell people, she would have set him straight in less than ten seconds with a stern look or a deep sigh.

Years later, when Lash Gorge Stratus was an adult and married, his father passed. He was at his father's bedside. It was the last time he cried. Leaus Perdu II's last words were spoken directly to his son.

You used to sing, he said.

Lash Gorge Stratus put his hand over his eyes to close them and kissed him on the forehead. Once his tears were gone, all he felt was rage and emptiness for those he had lost. The day after his father's death, at his own home, Alcee didn't recognize him. It was then when she realized that she had lost him though she fought to keep him as he was before. Lash Gorge Stratus knew that he had become lost, but he didn't do anything to try to stop it—he felt too uncomfortable recognizing himself. He wanted to forget all that he had remembered and continue to change into the man no one ever thought he would become. He was always good with handling physical pain, but when it came to the intangible hurt, he couldn't face it. He escaped into a world full of blood, power, money, and his eyes became redder and redder. Despite his wrongdoings, he remembered every loving moment, and it was the driving force to keep him away from all that he had known.

Vienna smiled and said she saw nothing but love. She kept talking about him and the man he used to be in the old stories she had heard about him. Lash Gorge Stratus's eyes became darker and redder—his being had become too complicated. He remembered that he had loved once, but it felt like such a distant memory now. I'm no longer myself, he thought.

He continued to point the pistol at Vienna's head, refusing to admit his memories. He squinted his eyes and tried hard not to remember the source of his rage. He tapped twice on the trigger making that dreadful sound that Vienna had recognized many times before while living on the streets. She continued to smile. He continued to point the pistol at her—one eye closed. Neither said anything.

Alcee and Sari had chopped down a tree and started to hollow it out. They were in a forest, bringing a variety of tools—axes, nails, hammers, bits and pieces of wood, and a metal instrument made by Cirrus Stratus used to carve different types of mediums. They were making a small boat. Drenched in sweat and breathing hard, they toiled and the boat was taking shape.

Cirrus Stratus could have made this in half the time and there are two of us, Alcee said. When it comes to making things, he has quite the talent. It could be a future profession of his.

She coughed and cleared her throat.

Even when he stole from people and stores, Alcee continued, he would bring them back and mold them into various tools and pieces of art.

Like Vienna, Sari said. I'm very interested in him. We've never met him, of course, but would very much like to. He has certainly caught Vienna's attention.

He has now certainly caught the whole town's attention, Alcee said.

They continued to work on the boat all day and the temperature decreased as the sun was going down, bringing a slight chill into the woods. Along with the breeze, they could hear a mumbling sound which resembled a neighing noise.

They both stopped working and stood and listened, trying to calm their breathing so they could better hear the sound in the winds.

It must be the ghost of the horses Cirrus Stratus killed for Vienna, Alcee said.

The sound became louder and louder, and the two ladies looked around expecting to see wild horses running by.

Perhaps they want their lives back, Alcee said. Perhaps they are forgiving him, or pleading us to find them.

Sari wiped the sweat off her brow and spat. She closed her eyes and took a deep breath.

Maybe they're trying to tell us the whereabouts of Cirrus Stratus and Vienna, she said.

Maybe, Alcee said. They will guide us. Let us finish our project.

They got back to work, listening to the neighing sounds of dead horses in the wind.

Cirrus

Stratus and his ghost stood under the sun, the sky full of soaring creatures. The smell of the ocean salt sauntered through the air. Just by his presence, the barren fields started to look more alive—there were spots of green grass forming, and the weeds turned into flowers.

It feels like you're changing, Cirrus Stratus the Ghost said.

I feel the same, Cirrus Stratus said. Where are we?

We are here, his ghost said. What you are doing has never been done before. You are special.

The ghost laughed.

I am special.

Cirrus Stratus heard a soft neighing traveling with a breeze. He looked out in the distance and saw two figures coming toward them.

Who are they? he asked.

Friends, Cirrus Stratus the Ghost said

The ghost picked up three clumps of hardened mud and started to juggle them.

As you are my ghost, Cirrus Stratus said, we are nothing alike.

The ghost continued to juggle.

We are very much the same, the ghost said. You just don't know me too well, yet.

The sun shone and the two figures continued to travel toward them, though Cirrus Stratus still couldn't recognize them. The skies were clear and full of the songs of birds.

Take away all of your rage and anger, Cirrus Stratus the

Ghost said. Take away all of your crimes and wrongdoings and you have me. I hope to be your future.

I've spent most of my life on the streets, Cirrus Stratus said. You know I'm an untouchable.

It's a wonderful life, the ghost said.

The streets are in my blood, Cirrus Stratus said. And everything I've done—yes, it was done with rage, but it was only for survival. I must look after my mother. She is the only way I know about compassion and giving. It's only us.

Oh, but there is someone else isn't there? Cirrus Stratus the Ghost said.

Cirrus Stratus sighed and his eyes glazed over. His ghost continued to juggle the clumps of dirt, whistling and humming, waiting for Cirrus Stratus to leave his daydream.

Vienna Vienna, Cirrus Stratus said. I've never felt this way, and I don't know what to do.

That's why I'm your ghost, he said. I'm here to help you.

At the same time, they both spoke the same words:

The world can be found inside Vienna. Her beauty, physically and spiritually, makes me forget about where I am now, where I was then, where I will be in the future.

The two figures were nearing them. Cirrus Stratus looked at them and drew a deep breath, lifting his head to the sky and letting the sun come down on his face—both the sun's soul and his own soul shone. Cirrus Stratus the Ghost started to glow as he continued to juggle.

Friends, Cirrus Stratus the Ghost said.

They must hate me, Cirrus Stratus said.

They understand, the ghost said. Go to them. Feel them. Talk to them.

The soft neighing became louder and louder though the sounds were still gentle and soothing, almost musical. The two horses came up to Cirrus Stratus and lowered their heads, nuzzling them against Cirrus Stratus's neck and chin. He sighed. There were tears coming down his face. Then there was crying, loud and soulful. He had let out of all the emotions he had kept restrained ever since he was a baby.

I'm so sorry, Cirrus Stratus said.

He lowered his neck and nuzzled the two horses.

I cannot remember the last time I cried, he said.

When you left your mother's stomach, Cirrus Stratus the Ghost said.

He stopped juggling and watched Cirrus Stratus apologize again to the horses—his voice muffled with tears and mucus.

I did it for love, Cirrus Stratus said.

The two horses started to lick his face, causing Cirrus Stratus to laugh.

Love, the ghost said. Love.

As Cirrus Stratus continued to nuzzle the horses, he could see more figures approaching in the distance. He knew there were more to come. This was just the beginning. The two horses continued neighing, sounding like they were accepting Cirrus Stratus's apologies, forgiving him. They started to trot away, and Cirrus Stratus waved bye to them, feeling better that he had been forgiven. He stood there waiting for the figures to approach. His ghost started to juggle again with clumps of dirt. They stood there as the sun shone, and there was a breeze. There were soaring birds, singing songs of love and sadness, reminding Cirrus Stratus of his mother. Pink-purple air. Cirrus Stratus couldn't recognize the solace in his blood—a feeling he hadn't felt since he was a child.

They're all dead, Cirrus Stratus the Ghost said.

Who are they? Cirrus Stratus asked.

They are the ones you have wronged and have since passed away, the ghost said. This is your chance to reconcile with them—the stealing, fighting, the vandalism, trouble, the rage and pure anger you've acted upon all these people.

Cirrus Stratus squinted as the figures approached. The first ghost held a cane, and his back was bent forward. He was bald and wore glasses—his skin wound tight against his bones. He walked up to Cirrus Stratus, breathing hard. Cirrus Stratus the Ghost continued to juggle.

I don't know you, Cirrus Stratus said.

I know you, the man said. I am Yoland Sabini Suarez.

But who are you? Cirrus Stratus said.

Cirrus Stratus the Ghost laughed and stopped juggling. He dropped the clumps of dirt and sat down crossed legged, pulling strands of grass and putting them in his mouth to chew. Cirrus Stratus bent down and pulled blades of grass, and started to chew them as well. Cirrus Stratus the Ghost, with his mouth full of grass, picked up his clumps of dirt and juggled them again while he remained sitting. Cirrus Stratus chewed the grass. He lost track of where he was for a moment—fixated on the grass, the sun, and his ghost, whose juggling was putting him into a trance.

Speak, Yoland Sabini Suarez said.

Cirrus Stratus spat some of the grass out and wiped his mouth. His voice became softer.

I'm sorry, Cirrus Stratus said. But I'm afraid I don't recognize you. I've done a lot of terrible things to a lot of people—too many faces.

You broke my windows and stole my vases. You urinated on my table and smeared blood all along my walls.

Cirrus Stratus's eyes became large.

I remember, he said.

He looked happy, excited that he could remember.

Don't be so happy, Yoland Sabini Suarez said. I very much detest you. Those vases belonged to my ancestors, passed on from generation to generation for centuries on end.

That's amazing, Cirrus Stratus said.

You ruined it all, Yoland Sabini Suarez said. I had nothing to leave to my children. They were my only valuable items.

Cirrus Stratus thought about that day. It was in the evening, and he was angry that he didn't have any coins to buy his mother a birthday gift. He was walking around the streets when he saw the vases through the windows of a blue and pink house. He used his elbows and fists to break through the windows to pocket the vases. He smeared the blood from his arms against the walls and urinated on the dinner table made of rich oak.

I also stole some necklaces, Cirrus Stratus said.

He went into a brief trance, envisioning the look on his mother's face as he gave her the vases. He smiled.

Those belonged to my wife, Yoland Sabini Suarez said.

He grunted and lifted his cane to strike Cirrus Stratus, who didn't flinch or budge.

Hit him, Cirrus Stratus the Ghost said.

He continued to juggle and whistle.

Hit me, Cirrus Stratus said. But do know I did it out of love. It's no excuse—I'm sorry.

Love, Yoland Sabini Suarez said.

His cane was still raised in the air, but he lost himself in the conversation, thinking about his wife and children.

I filled the vases with the ashes of a pigeon, Cirrus Stratus said. A pigeon both my mother and I loved, and in each vase, along with the ashes, I sprinkled crystals I had stolen from a jeweler. When we shook it, it sounded like the pigeon's song in the morning—a lovely song about love.

Love, Yoland Sabini Suarez repeated.

I meant well, Cirrus Stratus said.

Yoland Sabini Suarez left his trance and looked directly into Cirrus Stratus's eyes. Cirrus Stratus looked back. Yoland Sabini Suarez sighed, heaving his shoulders. He lowered his cane, and waved to them while walking away, following the horses' path. Cirrus Stratus looked on to the next figure as his ghost chewed grass and juggled.

Vienna

felt the top of the barrel of the pistol—its round shape pressed against her head. She kept her eyes open. She was smiling.

S**ari** and Alcee traveled in the canoe. The horses' neighs still strong in their heads, they followed the path of the voices and sweated. The sounds of the river in harmony with their breath, they paddled, not saying anything, saving their lungs for each stroke.

Lash

Gorge Stratus pressed the gun against Vienna's forehead. He couldn't get himself to pull the trigger as he was in and out of thinking about his wife and son. Vienna knew that he would lose himself in past worlds, so she continued to talk about it.

Your son, Vienna said. I've never met him, but I think I'm in love with him.

You will never see him, Lash Gorge Stratus said.

I will live to see him, Vienna said.

Perhaps, he said. Perhaps *he* is not alive.

You have good in you, Vienna said. I can see it.

Lash Gorge Stratus pushed the pistol harder against her forehead. There was nothing but the sounds of drips from the ceiling, forming a puddle, and the squeaks of rats huddled in the corners of the room.

I know all about your family, Vienna said. You were the greatest bowler of Dormier—you were the greatest bowler of the world.

Undefeated, Lash Gorge Stratus said.

And your parents, Vienna said. The greatest cooks of Dormier. Remember?

I will never remember, he said. Their blood and my blood are no longer the same. I am no longer the person they knew.

Remember, she said. I've talked to Alcee—she told me all about the love you once had.

With his pistol still against Vienna's head, he lit a cigar with his free hand and thought about flying kites with his son and his wife's singing, which he had always thought could put the world's twirl in reverse. He heard the notes of Alcee's piano—it brought him back to the mansion in the volcano, a place he hadn't seen since the falling out he had with his wife when entering into politics. The smell of eggplant curry from the kitchen, and the rose petals from the garden drifted around in his head. There was Cirrus Stratus sitting on a rug from the Eastern Half, playing with guitar strings and marbles. He thought about the nightly dinners and soirees—the cheese and wine, the salmon and soft hot bread, the waltzes and flowing gowns, the cigars and laughter, and sometimes Cirrus Stratus would still be awake, going from person to person, introducing himself and reciting poetry he had read or tried to write earlier that day. There was Alcee, twirling and twirling, making the world halt in its rotation—he saw her face and remembered how he fell in love with her.

They were young when they first met—both just finishing their 11th year in Upper Education. They went to different institutions but they encountered each other from time to time at local events. But it was one particular time when both Lash Gorge Stratus, or Leaus Perdu III back then, realized that he loved her.

They were at the beach—it was during winter, and they were the only two there, along with a few seagulls in the sky with their beaks holding urns. Leaus Perdu III was standing in the tides, with his slacks rolled up, embracing the cold and singing a song in his head. He didn't know that Alcee was there—she was walking along the damp sand, singing out loud. They were singing the same song. Leaus

Perdu III was in such a trance, he didn't hear Alcee, but she saw him standing in the lowering waves. She was surprised that somebody else was there as the beach was usually vacant during the cold season. Naked and full of soul, she walked up to Leaus Perdu III, continuing to sing the song. He finally heard her and opened his eyes and started to vocalize the song he had been singing in his head.

They stood there singing along with each other—they held hands, standing in the tides until the moon started to show. Alcee was shivering and Leaus Perdu III took off his shirt and slacks and gave them to her, helping her to keep warm. They sat in the sand all night long, bonding and sharing their lives and backgrounds and dreams. There were times of silence and she would put her head on his shoulder, both of them looking out into the ocean covered in moonbeams, listening to the songs of the tides. They stayed there until morning, and since that day, they had been in each other's minds.

The next day when they met at the coffee shop, Leaus Perdu III could not stop looking at her without smiling.

Why are you looking at me like that? Alcee asked him.

I know I'm in love with you, he said.

A week later, they were married. The ceremony was held on the beach—in the tides, during the evening. The ocean's song was their hymn and the seagulls were their witnesses.

Leaus Perdu III, as he transitioned into Lash Gorge Stratus, did not stop loving Alcee. He knew she still loved him, but after he lost her, his world became fueled with rage, power, and greed.

Cirrus

Stratus and the ghost stood in the middle of the plush green fields—the sun was up and bright, and there was a breeze that came through from time to time, causing the grass to sway from side to side. Cirrus Stratus had just finished reconciling with his last victim—a man he had fought and stole from during a burglary attempt at his mansion.

What now? Cirrus Stratus said.

He was smiling. What started off as a nightmare to him, had become a beautiful dream full of solace and meditation.

I can get used to living here, Cirrus Stratus said.

Cirrus Stratus the Ghost laughed.

Maybe in another lifetime, he said. Now, you must go back and fix the broken lives of the living.

Cirrus Stratus thought about his mother and Vienna. He thought about his estranged father, and all of the living beings with whom he had strife.

How do I go back? Cirrus Stratus said.

His ghost was walking in circles, causing the grass to be patted down, forming a circular path.

Your mother and a friend need help, the ghost said. You will find a way.

From underneath his shirt, the ghost pulled out a rusty spade—he started to toss it up and down. He smiled.

I'll see you around, the ghost said. You've done what others could not do. You survived living in the dead world. You made it come alive.

Cirrus Stratus looked around and saw all that was dead—all the tortured souls of a lost world—in a different tint. He saw potential in those who were on their hands and knees, shrieking and crying. He saw a light he had never seen before and ran toward it without looking back.

Goodbye, Cirrus Stratus the Ghost said. Looking forward to the future.

He vanished into the background. Cirrus Stratus continued to run toward the light. His body was in harmony—each thud of his steps was in beat with his breathing. His arms in fluid motion, Cirrus Stratus closed his eyes and ran.

When he opened his eyes, he found himself waking up in the middle of a whirlpool. The ocean was twirling, and Cirrus Stratus swam toward the top, fighting the swirling water. As he reached the surface, the force propelled him into the sky—he looked down below him and saw the green ocean below just before falling back into it, head first. He swam hard and tough toward a distant land. With each stroke, there was a grunt and a deep breath. His legs tore open the ocean and he reached the forest, drained and worn.

Lash

Gorge Stratus went to the woods and slept for four days straight. His gang, not knowing where he had gone, ransacked the town's businesses and homes in search of him. Dormier was in disarray—full of panic and fear as the torture continued for each day Lash Gorge Stratus was missing.

Vienna was still being kept in the basement of their headquarters, now blindfolded and lying on her side. She slept, for that was all she could do. She dreamt about Cirrus Stratus. Though she hadn't seen what he looked like, she dreamt that they were waltzing at a ball to a magnificent orchestra. He was wearing a tuxedo, and she was wearing a long green gown. She envisioned him being tan-skinned, slightly muscular with a strong jawline. She imagined intimate moments with Cirrus Stratus in her dreams, before opening her eyes, seeing nothing but the darkness of the cloth blindfolding her. She sighed—her skin warm and full of heat. Though her body, arms, and legs were bound tightly, she didn't struggle to get free. Her dreams freed her, and she closed her eyes again and imagined herself inside of a song she had never heard before.

When Lash Gorge Stratus woke up in the forest, on the roots of a wild banyan, he strangled a deer, and with red eyes, cooked and ate it as if he had just come out of a six month hibernation. He was in a stupor. Confused, tired, and hungry, he made his way through the woods. 800 trees away, Cirrus Stratus landed on the banks after swimming for two days with his eyes closed. He dragged himself ashore, breathing hard. His muscles were worn to their last bit of energy. Cirrus Stratus tried to stand up, but his legs wouldn't hold. Resting against some thick bushes, he sat patiently, waiting for his strength to come back.

Lash Gorge Stratus stumbled out of the woods into a clearing that led to Dormier. Before him, he saw an endless bronze and yellow field full of hay and ant piles. He looked up into the sky, and it made him feel empty—a sinking sensation filled his body. He took long breaths and continued to zigzag his way through the ant piles, trying his best not to fall down.

Cirrus Stratus stood up and stumbled, traveling through the forest in random diagonal movements from one tree to another. Sometimes he kept his eyes closed, using his arms to guide himself. With his face covered in red lines from the branches striking his face, he made it to the clearing and saw a figure in the distance. Cirrus Stratus called out to him, in search of some kind of help to gain his bearings. He called out again. Lash Gorge Stratus barely heard his voice. He turned around and squinted, seeing Cirrus Stratus's figure, but he couldn't tell that it was his son. He grunted and turned back around, continuing to stagger toward the city.

Cirrus Stratus called out again. He tried to run toward Lash Gorge Stratus, but his legs didn't have the energy. He thought about his ghost and his time in the land that didn't exist.

I should have stayed back, Cirrus Stratus said.

He heard his ghost's voice.

But you are not done yet, the ghost said. There is plenty more to do.

He kept walking. As he looked at the figure ahead, he saw him falling down.

The whirlpool that thrusted Cirrus Stratus out was the same

whirlpool Sari and Alcee found themselves twirling around inside, battling the waters. They didn't see Cirrus Stratus as they were occupied in dealing with the whirlpool, and when Cirrus Stratus fell back down into the ocean after being propelled from the currents, he was too far away to notice.

Sari and Alcee, sore and naked and breathless, were struggling hard to find a way out of the whirlpool, but the strong circular currents wouldn't let them out. They tried to shout at each other to form a plan of escape, but between the sounds of the whirling and the bobbing in and out of the water, they couldn't understand each other.

When she was under the water, Alcee would look up and see the ocean roof glowing, lit from the sun above—it looked magical to her, and she thought how beautiful it would be if this was the last image she saw before dying.

Sari would look down when she was underwater—noticing the drifting particles of ocean plants and various multicolored ocean life. Each time she would go under, she would speak into the water, saying "pretty" to all that she noticed. One time, she saw a red and yellow fish with bright blue stripes looking at her. Sari pushed her hand against the water to wave hello, and with bubbles leaving her mouth, she said, This is all so wonderful. The fish full of color stayed in place, moving its tail back and forth, and continued to look at Sari. She imagined that the fish wished it could help them, but it was too small to do anything.

Soon after, the fish swam away, and Sari and Alcee were at the water's surface, finally able to communicate with each other.

Should we jump out? Sari asked.

Alcee was trying to situate herself in the canoe to handle the currents.

Let's stay, she said. Let's go with the water and sink ourselves and swim out of it.

Yes, Sari said. Try to keep hold of the canoe while we're underwater.

And we'll guide ourselves out of it underwater, Alcee said.

They closed their eyes and plunged into the vortex of the whirlpool. They were thrown about while in the center of the swirl, but they held on tight, and once they made it through the foamed tornado, they opened their eyes— both seeing a red and yellow fish with bright blue stripes. Alcee imagined that it was smiling. Behind the fish, were two large dolphins. With bubbles coming out of her mouth, Alcee said, thank you.

The two dolphins took over. Sari and Alcee got on their backs with the canoe held in between them and they throttled through the water until the whirlpool was behind them. Sari and Alcee were on the surface of the ocean again, shifting themselves into the canoe. The dolphins and the small fish swam a circle around them before leaving.

Thanks, Alcee said.

What should we do? Sari said. Where are we?

We are where we should be, Alcee said. Let's row.

And they did.

Alejo sat alone in the dining room eating a dinner Thuroon had prepared for him: lentils and rice with cauliflower, carrots, broccoli, and a portion of lamb. He sat there in a suit, sweating, softly chewing his meal. There was a quiet rage still inside of him—Sari, Vienna, his horses, Cirrus Stratus, the disappearance of Lash Gorge Stratus—and he felt a strange energy coming from Thuroon. He had been especially nice to Alejo, cooking his favorite meals, performing his duties at the mansion with an unusual vigor, sparking conversations, and working extra hours.

Thuroon was in the kitchen cleaning and washing the pots and pans—he was thinking about a way to tell Alejo that he would be leaving. He was sweating and nervous—he wanted to tell him that night. The thought of being free from Alejo's wrath made him hopeful. He went into the dining room and asked Alejo how he was doing. Alejo had savored each flavor, each bite—his taste buds were in full bloom. He had closed his eyes each time his fork entered his mouth, and after he finished each bite, he sighed. He didn't reveal this to Thuroon.

Sir, Thuroon said.

What? Alejo said. I want to be left alone.

I was just wondering, how is dinner?

Whatever, Alejo said.

Sir, Thuroon said.

It's okay, he said.

Thank you, sir, Thuroon said.

Your cooking is mediocre, Alejo said.

He took another bite and sighed, closing his eyes.

Horrible, he said.

My apologies, Thuroon said.

What's wrong with you? Alejo replied.

Sir, Thuroon said. I'm trying my best.

You're lucky, he said. You're blessed that you're still working for me.

Thank you, sir, Thuroon said.

He walked back into the kitchen, and Alejo, sweating from the spices, his collared shirt drenched, took another bite and closed his eyes. He sighed. Alejo's state of mind made Thuroon doubtful about turning in his resignation that night. He felt threatened, uneasy, and he worried about how Alejo would react to his resignation.

Servant, Alejo said.

Thuroon walked back into the dining room.

Sir, he said.

This is nowhere near your best, Alejo said. It's nearer to your worst. It's all so bland. So bland.

My apologies, Thuroon said.

He turned back around to leave the room and turned back around again, facing Alejo

Sir, Thuroon said.

He took a long breath. His body was at unease, trying hard not to walk in circles or shuffle about.

Leave me alone, Alejo said.

Sir, Thuroon said.

Sir, sir, sir, Alejo mocked. You're such a miserable thing. I should have left you in the gutters. You deserve nothing.

I am sorry, Thuroon said.

Alejo hesitated before pushing his plate aside.

I hope there isn't any dessert, he said. I can't bear anymore of this horrible cooking.

Now Thuroon wanted to let out his resentment toward Alejo. He wanted to leave there and then and never come back. He wanted to be with his family and go back to the gutters where he happily worked.

May I have another chance to redeem myself? Thuroon said.

Alejo stared at the plate he had just pushed aside, missing those last few bites.

You're such trash, he said. Every morning I wake up and laugh at you. You disgust me.

Thuroon bowed his head.

My sincere apologies, he said. I mean not to disgust you.

It would be healthy both for you and your family if you continue to work for me, Alejo said.

He grunted.

I have made some mango mousse for dessert, Thuroon replied.

Alejo grunted again.

Give it, he said.

Thuroon went back to the kitchen, thinking about what Alejo had said about his family. Was it a threat? he wondered, and does he know that I wanted to resign? His patience was reaching its limit. When he came back to the dining room, he noticed that Alejo had finished off the last bites of his dinner—the plate he had pushed aside earlier was now completely empty. He didn't look Thuroon in the eyes, looking like a guilty dog knowing it had done something wrong. Thuroon put the mango mousse in front of him.

Sir, Thuroon said. What did you mean when you were talking about the health of my family?

Alejo took his first bite and closed his eyes while lifting his head up toward the ceiling.

I know a lot of people, he said. People you won't like, but they can take care of anything I wish them to do.

Thuroon wanted to leave without saying a word, to never come back, to move away so he would never be reached by Alejo again. His patience turned into a rage he had never felt before. He was never the violent type—since he was a child, he was always kind and gentle. Even working in the sewers didn't harden his mentality. His parents, who had passed away, had brought him up with such care, he knew nothing else but love and nonviolence. He had never gotten into a fight or an argument—always forgiving, always patient, but Alejo had tested his true being. He was new to this feeling of anger—so new that he didn't know what to do with it. He had never spoken or thought of any kind of ill will toward anyone—his genuine personality, his purity and love for happiness, didn't allow it. Alejo had pushed his boundaries to the fullest, making him feel uncomfortable and scared. But Thuroon didn't give in to his anger. He thought about his children and his wife and calmed. His solace didn't exist in himself but more so in those he loved. Perhaps it was the time to say that he had enough—perhaps he should say all that he wanted to say to Alejo, or maybe even to start a fight that he had once dreamt about. He bowed his head and closed his eyes, breathing in hard. He exhaled and opened his eyes and smiled.

Sir, he said. I am very thankful.

For what, Alejo said, your miserable life?

He took another bite of the mousse, trying hard not to reveal his affinity for Thuroon's dessert. Thuroon stood there quietly, waiting for Alejo to finish his last bite. Once he was done, he picked up his plate and took his time washing it. Alejo went to the recreational room and smoked a cigar while looking into a lit fireplace.

I am going back home, Thuroon said. I'll be back tomorrow before the sun rises. Alejo didn't acknowledge him—he continued to puff on his cigar, tilting his head to the side. Thuroon waited for a moment before leaving, smiling as he thought about home. After he left, Alejo spoke to himself in a trance.

Goodbye, he said.

Sari and Alcee made it to land. They didn't know where they were, but they were relieved to be back on solid ground. They kissed the dirt and looked up at the sky, giving long sighs. Naked and wet, they rubbed their bodies against bark to warm up.

Where are we? Sari wondered.

We're still alive, Alcee said.

Sari tore off twigs and large leaves and wrapped them around her waist. Alcee did the same, and they started walking along the banks, hoping to meet someone fishing or traveling in the waters.

They walked for five miles until they saw someone standing in the river's current. He was shirtless, and the waters came up to his stomach as he stood there with his fishing line. Alcee called out to him. He waved and shouted.

Catfish, he said.

Where are we? Sari asked.

Catfish, the man repeated.

Sari walked into the water to meet him, causing the twigs and leaves around her waist to fall off and drift with the current. The man's eyes became large and round. He only spoke in one word sentences, as he wasn't a man of formal language—more of a man of doing. He revealed a huge smile, showing bright white teeth.

Here, he said.

Standing close to him, Sari found the man attractive—a strong, thick mustache, long wavy black hair coming down from under his tan bowl hat, his muddy body revealing muscles up and down his arms and neck. He was still smiling, tipping his hat to her. He looked around.

Where? he said.

Sari looked around with him.

Yes, she said. Where?

It's evening, the fisherman said.

His hands were still holding the reel, subconsciously fishing, waiting for a tug.

Very much so, Sari said. And where are we this evening?

The fisherman nodded his head. His smile was relentless, never-ending. It humbled Sari. She realized that he was gentle, simple in the sense that he viewed the world and communicated in a way that was full of kindness. Sari understood this and appreciated his humility—his simplicity and gentle manner. Perhaps, he didn't know how to speak well, Sari thought. Or perhaps, she thought, he knew the language too well and knew what words to use to convey his messages.

What is your name? she asked him. I am Sari.

He tipped his hat to her again.

Pablo, he said.

Would you happen to know how to get to the city of Dormier from here? she asked.

Pablo nodded his head, still smiling.

Dormier, he repeated.

Sari looked at his muscles again—neat and tight around his arms. His chest slightly protruded over his defined stomach.

Follow, he said.

Just as he was about to walk toward the banks, his reel jerked, and Pablo pulled back, keeping his fishing line intact. He pulled out a large catfish. Turning around to Sari, his smile became even bigger. Sari couldn't help but to laugh.

Come, he said.

Alcee met them in the middle of the water to make sure everything was okay, and they walked back to the banks of the river. There was a path in the forest, and Pablo led them to a clearing where a town could be seen in the distance.

Pablo had a campsite in the clearing. He started to gut the fish, still smiling. Sari and Alcee watched and waited. When he was finished, he started a fire.

Eat, he said. Yours.

It was not until then that Sari and Alcee realized the emptiness in their stomachs, and they could not deny his offer. They spoke little and once the fish was cooked, only the sounds of chewing could be heard. Pablo himself didn't eat, as he wanted to make sure Sari and Alcee had enough food. Once they finished, Pablo stood up and picked up their tin plates to wash them. His smile never left his face. He pulled out some blankets and gave them to Sari and Alcee. He had only one pillow, but it was large enough for both of them to sleep on.

Rest, Pablo said.

He fixed their blankets on a soft patch of leveled land.

Tomorrow, he said.

Tomorrow, Sari said.

She realized that she fell into a trance as she looked into his eyes or watched him working quietly, his smile never leaving. She felt overwhelmed with a sense of passion she hadn't felt before.

Dormier, he said.

We are so grateful, Alcee said. Forever thankful.

Stars, Pablo said.

Sari and Alcee looked up and saw the night sky glittered with dots of light. Sari couldn't tell if she was just delusional from exhaustion or if it was genuine emotion, but with each second she spent with Pablo, the more she became enamored with the man who never stopped smiling. As they stared into the night, silent except the sounds of the forest creatures, they fell asleep. Pablo, who had given all of his blankets away, made a mound of dirt to use as a pillow and slept without any covers.

When they awoke, Pablo had breakfast already made for them. He went early to catch the morning fish and was able to get a good amount. Soon after, Sari and Alcee followed Pablo to the town just after the clearing. With rest and nourishment, Sari still realized that she had the same emotions for Pablo as she did the day before. Alcee could tell by the way she looked and acted around him that Sari was enchanted with Pablo. No longer naked, as they were wearing Pablo's spare clothes, Sari was trying her best to fix her appearance as much as possible. They whispered to each other as they followed Pablo, talking about their new acquaintance.

But he doesn't even speak, Alcee said.

He says what needs to be said, Sari said.

But how could one argue with someone like that?

He is not one who argues.

He never stops smiling, Alcee went on.

It's such a warming smile, Sari said.

You're in love, Alcee said.

So be it, Sari agreed. A strange feeling.

Pablo stopped and pointed at the town as it was not too far away.

What is it called? Alcee asked.

Mourir, Pablo said.

Pretty name, Sari said.

Pablo continued to smile.

Come, he said.

Once they reached the city, Sari and Alcee noticed the streets full of markets and food huts—small makeshift shops full of people. The town smelled of fresh bread, bacon, eggs, and maple syrup. Pablo continued to walk through the town, which was quite a small one, for soon they arrived at the end and reached a small hut similar to those where the untouchables lived in Dormier. He took out a tin can underneath a pile of clutter—pitchers, plates, cups, cutlery, and took out some coins.

Please, Pablo said. Sit. Back.

They sat and talked—Pablo left, only to come back soon after with fresh bread, cheese, fruits and vegetables. He put them in a satchel and gave it to them.

Come, he said.

They left the hut and Pablo led them out of the city to a nearby forest—the forest that connected to Dormier. He pointed.

Straight, Pablo said.

Dormier, Sari said.

His smile was there. He nodded.

Thanks, Pablo said.

He stuck out his hand again, pointing toward the forest.

Alcee and Sari thanked him repeatedly, and Pablo just smiled and kept nodding his head, saying thanks to them each time they said it. They looked at the forest with their eyes shining, knowing home is on the other side. However, at the same time, they realized that their journey to find Cirrus Stratus was unsuccessful, and they didn't know how Dormier was doing under the growing power of Lash Gorge Stratus's rage. Sari turned around and faced Pablo. She hugged him and put her lips close to his ear.

One day I will come back and find you, she said. And I will kiss you.

Pablo continued to smile.

Thanks, he said.

With a satchel of food and blankets in hand, they walked toward the forest. Pablo watched them until they disappeared. Before entering the forest, Sari turned around and waved, not knowing if Pablo could see her. Pablo waved back.

Bye, he said.

He walked back into his hut and sat on the stone floor.

Sari, he said.

Cirrus

Stratus was nearing Lash Gorge Stratus, who was still having trouble standing up—weak and delusional and covered in sweat, he kept on thinking about his past life. Full of torment and nostalgia, his memories broke down into moments from childhood to when his family fell apart—the first time he caught a bass with his father under a frozen sun; when he and Alcee were building their house in the valley on their own and taking breaks to dance and bowl on the rough terrain; the time when Cirrus Stratus tried to fly toward the sky and fell off the roof, spraining both ankles, limping his way to the house to get back on the roof only to be caught by him.

You look hurt, he said.

I tried to get to the clouds from the roof, Cirrus Stratus said.

And what happened? his father asked.

I fell to the ground, he said. Hurt my ankles.

And so you're trying again, the father said, despite what happened?

If I don't try again and again, Cirrus Stratus asked, how will I learn?

Leaus Perdu III couldn't help but smile to hear such a statement from his six year old son. He went to the roof with Cirrus Stratus.

Are you going to try too? Cirrus Stratus asked.

Of course, Leaus Perdu III said. How else can I learn to fly with you?

Cirrus Stratus hugged his father's leg and then both looked up at the clouds.

If only we were kites, the son said.

He turned toward his father with one hand tugging on his waist coat.

To meet the clouds, he continued. It would be quite a greeting.

Again, Leaus Perdu III smiled and laughed.

I would love to meet the inside of your head, he said. To see your thoughts second by second.

They both turned again to face the edge of the roof. The end of the volcano, its rim, could be seen in the distance. They jumped as high as they could and dropped straight down, hitting the ground—Leaus Perdu III sprained both his wrists, while Cirrus Stratus bruised his whole side. However, neither yelped in pain or screamed. They both stood up, brushing themselves off and looked at each other. Cirrus Stratus smirked, and his father did the same. They looked up at the roof again and made their climb without saying a word to each other. But as they were climbing the side, they each felt a hand grasp their legs, pulling them back down to the ground. Alcee, looking angry as ever, pulled them by the ears, leading them inside.

Idiots, she said. My lovely idiots.

The pain from having their ears pulled was worse than the pain from dropping to the ground from the roof. Both yelping, they were told to sit down in the living room. Alcee scolded both of them—Cirrus Stratus had never seen his mother so angry before. He listened quietly to her, not wanting to make direct eye contact with her, but Alcee demanded that he look at her.

Face what you fear, she said.

Alcee paced back and forth, continuing to scold them with her arms flailing about. Her husband was trying his best to hide a grin as he marveled at her, thinking that she looked so beautiful in her anger, a side of her he had never seen as well.

I will slap you so hard, Alcee said. Your head will go round and round until it falls off.

You're pretty, Leaus Perdu III said. The way your nose wrinkles and your face blushes. The way you're in total control, knowing every word to say without hesitation. I love you.

He put his hand on Cirrus Stratus's shoulder.

We both love you, the father said.

I love you mother, Cirrus Stratus said. I promise not to try to fly to the clouds again.

Alcee tried her best to hold onto her anger but she couldn't help lightening up, releasing the tension from her forehead, neck, and jaw.

What am I to do with you all? she said.

With an exclamation, Leaus Perdu III jumped up from the sofa.

Love us, he said. Come. I will make enchiladas and potato waffles.

Cirrus Stratus hopped up in excitement and ran straight to the kitchen. Leaus Perdu III walked up to Alcee and put his hands on her shoulders.

Idiot, she said.

Your idiot, he said.

He kissed her on the forehead.

Let us waltz, he said. To the music that exists in our heads.

They held hands and moved around the room in silence, as if an orchestra was loud and crisp in their minds—as if they had been dancing since infinity. Leaus Perdu III whispered to Alcee.

I am forever humbled to be in your presence, he said.

Cirrus Stratus reached Lash Gorge Stratus in the clearing that led to Dormier. As soon as he realized that the figure was his father, he spat on him and kicked him in the stomach as he was trying to stand up again.

Roof, Lash Gorge Stratus said.

He was coming back to reality, shifting to his side as his hands covered his stomach. He looked up at his son.

You failed, Cirrus Stratus said. I am back. My exile is no longer.

Lash Gorge Stratus was vulnerable—a feeling he hadn't known in years.

My son, he said.

Cirrus Stratus spat on him again—it landed on his face. But as he was about to kick him for the second time, he had a vision—a vision that brought him back to his exile in the land that didn't exist. He saw his own ghost, juggling three strands of hay, while whistling a tune his mother would hum when she would put him to sleep. He saw himself there, in the land of the ghosts, being reminded of humility and compassion. He stuck his foot back onto the grass, refraining from kicking his father again.

You're no good, Cirrus Stratus said.

I once was, Lash Gorge Stratus said.

You were once my father, Cirrus Stratus said.

What am I now? Lash Gorge Stratus asked.

Just a little child, his son answered.

Lash Gorge Stratus coughed and wheezed, still trying to get his breath from being kicked. Cirrus Stratus kicked him again—he couldn't help it, his rage growing, causing his father to roll over. He managed to get some words out between his gasps for breath.

Remember when—, Lash Gorge Stratus began.

Cirrus Stratus gritted his teeth and started to kick dirt all over him, spitting on him too. He didn't want to remember when—he had too much scorn for the man who used to be his father. Again, he thought about his time in exile. Feeling humbled, he suddenly stopped. Looking down at his father, he had never seen him so vulnerable and weak. With his family, or in politics, in all of his greed and fighting, he had always been a confident man— even when his parents passed away, he never showed any vulnerability. Now, he looked like a homeless man, void of nourishment and strength. His eyes were fading. He looked like an untouchable.

Remember when, Lash Gorge Stratus said again.

He was on all fours, trying to stand up.

Remember when, Cirrus Stratus said. Remember when you left my mother—your wife—and your son? Remember when you started assaulting the town of Dormier, stuffing cucumbers down people's throats, burning houses and buildings, stealing and bullying?

As he spoke, the rage within Cirrus Stratus grew, almost making him kick his father again. However, he refrained from doing so as he kept seeing visions of his own ghost in the barren lands of the tormented.

Remember when? he continued. Remember when you threatened the lives of those who loved you most? Remember when you took from those who didn't have anything, or when you burned the town's crops just before the harvest? You searched for power and money through your greed and rage, yet you are nothing but a little baby.

Cirrus Stratus didn't kick him, but he put his foot on the side of his body, while Lash Gorge Stratus was still on his knees, and pushed, causing him to topple over again.

Vienna was still on her side on the damp concrete, blindfolded. In and out of sleep, and starving, she tried her best to imagine Cirrus Stratus. She dreamt about meeting him in the forest where had kept the two dead horses for her, and then walking along the banks, listening to the sounds of the river. She dreamt about holding hands. She saw herself laughing and eating dinner with Cirrus Stratus. Every now and then, she would talk out loud to grasp reality—to let herself know that she was still alive.

She counted the drips of water coming down from the ceiling—but when she would reach around 400, she would lose her concentration and start all over again. Not having anything to drink in days, she cupped her hand and let some of the drips gather in her palms before licking them to help quench her thirst. It wasn't a substantial amount, but it was enough to keep her body from going into shock.

Although she couldn't see the rats, she could hear their squeaks. She had conversations with them, who were huddled in the far corner of the room.

What do you like to eat? she asked.

Vienna imagined what they would say.

Well, the rats said all at once, we absolutely love fried eggs and gouda.

And okra, one rat said in a high pitched voice.

That sounds delicious, Vienna said. And maybe some Havarti on salmon. I had it once and it was wonderful.

And maybe, the rats said. And maybe some, and maybe some cauliflower and potatoes.

They sounded excited.

Yes, Vienna said.

She was equally excited.

My mother makes a great curry, she said.

Where is your mother? the rats said.

I don't know, she said. I'm sure she's looking for me.

Why is she looking for you? they said.

Because I've been kidnapped by Lash Gorge Stratus, she said. I don't want to be here.

Oh, the rats said. He's so rude. He never gives us any food and sometimes he kills some of our family members.

He does the same with humans, Vienna said.

We will help you, the rats said

Vienna was brought back to reality with the feeling of teeth on her wrists and legs, nibbling the rope that bound her. Too weak and tired, she fell asleep dreaming about fried eggs, gouda and curry. When she woke up, she realized that she was no longer tied up. Her first attempt at standing up was unsuccessful, as she couldn't get her bearings or strength situated. The second attempt was successful. She stretched her legs and rubbed her wrists. She took off her blindfold and saw the rats huddled together in the opposite corner. Not too far away from them was a round tin container.

Still not knowing if this was all a dream or if this was real, she gathered the rats and put them in the tin box. Walking out the door, she saw a dimly-lit hallway—one way was ended by a wall, so she went the other way, passing by several doors until she reached a large room. She peered in and saw that it was empty. Just beyond the room was a foyer and the front door. She looked around—the room was bare except for a few chairs and one table. With the box of rats in hand, Vienna ran as fast as she could out to the front door—she kept running without looking back, hoping that no one was following her. Once she reached familiar territory, she slowed down to catch her breath. The world looked surreal to her. Knowing not to go back to her hut where she could easily be found, she hid in an alley while thinking of where to properly hide.

As Sari and Alcee traveled through the forest, Alcee thought about her mother, Amelia. She was a prominent sculptor in her time, commissioned by the mayor or other highly ranked politicians from around the world, including the Ambassador of the Oceans. She had spent days upon days working in her studio, never leaving until she finished that particular piece. Her father, Bovarda Couza LaMachelle, who was a brilliant math teacher adored by his students and peers, retired early from his profession to stay at home with Alcee as Amelia worked on her sculptures.

Alcee was quite close to her parents, though she didn't see her mother too much. She would have random memories of being with her—even if it was only for a small amount of time, they were moments that made such a significant impact on her life, even the way she herself parented. One of her most memorable moments was when she was a child, searching for turtles in a ditch, and a tree fell on top of her, trapping her leg.

Alcee could do nothing but shout and shout as much as she could for help. Her voice traveled with the winds and Amelia heard her while fertilizing the soil on their property. She followed the voice to the ditch until she found Alcee.

Without saying a word, Amelia lifted the tree as if it was as light as a tea cup and Alcee crawled away from underneath. No bones were broken, but her thigh and knee were already bruising, and she was crying from the pain.

What happened? Amelia asked.

I was searching for turtles, Alcee said.

Did you find any?

Not even one, Alcee said.

Keep looking, her mother said.

Alcee stood up and limped around—her mother helped her look, too. They walked inside of the ditch, looking under fallen branches and leaves. Amelia finally found one tucked in a mound of dirt but instead of pulling it out for Alcee, she pretended to twist her ankle, falling down. She yelped in pain, and Alcee limped toward her as fast as she could.

I think I tripped over this mound of dirt, Amelia said.

I'll help you up, Alcee said.

With all her might, and a slight grimace, she pulled her mother up to her feet and then looked at the mound of dirt. She saw the turtle and shouted in joy.

Mother, she said. Mother. Mother—look.

She pulled out the turtle, holding it up high for her mother to see.

Wow, Amelia said. It's beautiful.

She looked at her daughter and saw the sparkle in her eyes—so happy, it almost made Amelia cry. Alcee ran her hand across its shell—the turtle, neither defensive nor scared, kept its head out, and Alcee rubbed her fingertips under its mouth.

Come, Amelia said. Let us both limp back home, and we'll make some chocolate beignets.

Alcee jumped up and down in joy before stopping in pain, making Amelia laugh. She put the turtle back where she found it, telling it goodbye.

What's its name? Amelia said.

Alcee closed her eyes, thinking of a name.

Wilder Cane, she said.

She took her mother's hand and they walked back home—Alcee limped, and Amelia pretended to limp.

Moments like those thrived in Alcee's memories. She was a lady of the past—whether it was with her parents or with her son and husband.

They steadily trekked through the forest, anxious about getting back to Dormier. Alcee sparked conversations, but Sari's mind wandered off, thinking about her recent acquaintance, Pablo from Mourir.

In contrast, Sari was not one of memories. Her demeanor either consisted of living in the present or thinking about the future. She was one of anticipation more than anything else. Her past experiences made her this way, and in turn, it made Vienna that way as well. Sari didn't have too many memories of her family's past—she had no family. All that she was concerned with was making sure that she and Vienna could make it from one day to the next, as was the life of an untouchable.

She didn't know her parents—she was born on the streets, found by two mongrels in an alley of one of the streets where the untouchables lived. The two dogs didn't leave her sight at first, gently pressing their bodies against her to keep her warm, but they realized that she was hungry and one would leave to find scraps of food. Vienna couldn't eat any solid food, as she was just a newly born baby, and the two mongrels couldn't find a way to get the food into her mouth for her to properly digest. The dogs, sensing that the baby would die of starvation, barked incessantly, in hopes that someone would hear them and find the baby.

The untouchables, so accustomed to hearing a variety of street noises including the barking of stray dogs, didn't give the mongrels in the alley any attention. One night though, they started howling, realizing that the baby was nearing death. They howled and howled with such intensity that their plea finally became noticed by some of the untouchables nearby. They were of no help, however, for as soon as they saw the baby, they ran away, not wanting the burden of an additional body to care for when they were already in poor situations themselves.

The mongrels, in desperation, ventured off—one sniffed out a milk satchel from one of the huts. Without hesitation, it snatched the milk bag with its mouth and hurried back to the alley, meeting the other mongrel and Sari. They tried to get the tip of the satchel into Sari's mouth but the baby wouldn't take the tip of the satchel. The dogs started to howl again. One of the mongrels, with a strong instinct for motherhood, put her nipples over Sari's mouth and it worked. She was fed from dog's milk—a baby born of the streets and nourished by mongrels from the same streets, and this was how Sari survived the first few months of being abandoned amongst the untouchables.

From the milk of a mongrel, she became a true untouchable. Her upbringing taught her humility, caring, and kindness, though it easily could have taught her completely the opposite. It made her view the world in another way—with compassion, whether it was in spite or because of the way she survived on the streets. She saw the sky as opportunity, and she saw the streets as her loving home, and she saw people, whether they lived in straw huts or in mansions, with a love that can't be described. Her gritty life of prostitution and violence didn't change her perception of how she viewed reality. It was always full of hope, light, and the gleam of being.

When Vienna came into her life, she was a nurturing mother, caring for her just as the mongrels had—simply a pure soul looking over another. She devoted all of her love, time, and attention to her daughter. She did whatever she needed to do to take care of the most beloved person in her life.

She saw her daughter as an angel, yet at the same time, she herself became somewhat surreal while nurturing her daughter. Though she had been a prostitute living on the streets, many eventually came to admire her and respect her for the way she carried herself and looked after her daughter. With Vienna in her life, she learned how to control her own world. Even when Lash Gorge Stratus came into power, and despite her occasional worry, she was always hopeful, and she wouldn't let anyone get in her way of Vienna living a happy life.

Cirrus

Stratus looked at his father, not knowing what to do. He was confused as to whether he should continue to kick him, help him up, or to just leave him as he was and go back to Dormier.

Lash Gorge Stratus kept talking to him, asking him questions about the past, about when he was just a child and when they were a family. However, Cirrus Stratus didn't answer any of his questions. He remained pensive, but he also didn't want his father to affect the way he acted.

He bent down and ran his hands through the grass, pulling some out and holding it up to his nose before putting it in his mouth to taste earth. He scraped the dirt with his fingers as if he was digging for the core of the earth. He looked at the dirt tucked in neatly under his fingernails.

Untouchables, he said.

He looked at his father with watery eyes, goosebumps and a headache.

I loved you father, he said.

Cirrus Stratus started walking again toward Dormier, leaving his father as he was—weak, vulnerable, oblivious. On his way back home, his mind was deluged with the past—thinking about Leaus Perdu III and Alcee when they were together as husband and wife. He tried to not let the sentiment get the best of him but he was still just a young man in search of happiness and love. His eyes were large and round, tearing up—he continued to walk, thinking about pancakes, kites, music and soirees. It was a feeling he hadn't felt since becoming an untouchable.

I once was, he thought. We once were.

Lash Gorge Stratus, alone again in the fields with his delirium, couldn't help but tear up as well—red eyes once full of scorn and greed had temporarily shifted to red eyes full of sadness and remorse.

He thought about the time when he, his wife and son were leaving the bakery one evening when they were met by an untouchable trying to mug them. Cirrus Stratus, no taller than his father's knees, stood in front of his parents, telling the mugger, try your best to get to them. However, Alcee and Leaus Perdu III, being sympathetic and kind, gave the untouchable money and the bread they had bought at the bakery.

Eat, Alcee said. And find some good use with these coins.

That's all I wanted, the untouchable said. I didn't want to do this but I have three children and a wife who are starving. My apologies.

We understand, Leaus Perdu III said.

He picked up Cirrus Stratus and held him against his body as Alcee gave the man all they had on them—coins, food, jewelry. The untouchable was quite humbled by his actions.

It wasn't always like this, he said. One day I will help you. My name is Egrette Roose Flounder, and I am forever grateful. You just saved my family for the time being.

We are happy to help, Leaus Perdu III said.

Egrette bowed his head and thanked them. He took the food and money and left.

Thuroon hadn't left Alejo—he had been working diligently every day, accepting Alejo's snide comments and continuing his duties.

Alejo himself was in disarray: Lash Gorge Stratus was missing and Vienna had escaped. Both his anger and love for her hadn't lessened— if anything, both increased as the days passed. His search parties had given up, thinking that either Lash Gorge Stratus had left Dormier, or was kidnapped or killed by his enemies who spanned untouchables, the opposing political party, or anyone else who had fallen under Lash Gorge Stratus's rage.

Alejo didn't give up; he continued to search by himself, ransacking house after house, store after store, and interrogating any possible suspects to find any kind of information about the whereabouts of Lash Gorge Stratus. He also searched for Vienna, trying to find where she was hiding, but no one had any information about the two. He wanted her in his control—he wanted to know where she was at every moment, and not knowing this left him feeling like he had no control over his own world.

After one day of searching, Alejo came home to find Thuroon on his hands and knees scrubbing the base of the living room walls with a rag and vinegar. Alejo snorted.

Good sir, Thuroon said. Good evening.

You're such a pathetic servant, Alejo said.

Yes sir, Thuroon said.

Alejo walked into his study, lighting a cigar. He saw that most of his books in the study were thrown all over the place, some destroyed—their spines split or pages torn out, and some were in the fireplace, half-ashed. He shouted for his servant. Thuroon tucked his rag into his pants and went into the study to see Alejo pacing back and forth, cursing and mumbling.

What is this? Alejo demanded. What happened here? What did you do?

The night before, Thuroon witnessed Alejo throwing a drunken fit, heaving his books and tearing and burning them in a rage. He was talking to himself and cursing everything and everyone. Alejo had no recollection of doing so, assuming that Thuroon ransacked the room for revenge.

Sir, Thuroon said.

He couldn't help but to chuckle.

You did this last night.

Don't lie to me, Alejo said. Don't blame me for your actions. Liar.

You were drunk, Thuroon said. You might not remember.

Alejo picked up one of the broken books and threw it at his servant. Thuroon shifted his body to dodge it. He noticed Alejo's red eyes—full of rage and confusion.

Sir, Thuroon said. I promise. I'm telling no lies. This is the truth. I promise.

Promise, Alejo said. Your promise is nothing but a stray cat's urine.

Sir, Thuroon said. Perhaps a stray cat's urine is full of truth. How would we know?

Gutter feces, Alejo said. You came from the sewage and now you're arguing with me. Speaking philosophy now, are you? So wise and smart, aren't you? I can end you in a moment's notice. How's that for cat's urine?

Why would you do such a thing? Thuroon asked.

Because you're nothing, he said. You're a nuisance. A dumb, stupid nuisance, an overgrown delinquent.

Sir, Thuroon said, why do you still employ me? Why have you kept me around all this time?

Thuroon was hoping that instead of having to resign, that Alejo would terminate him instead.

Feeling bold, are you? Alejo said. All of a sudden you're trying to be human, with feelings and opinions.

To Thuroon's surprise, Alejo started to dance around the room, singing to himself. He ran into small tables and vases and other displays that were in front of him, forgetting that he was in the middle of a conversation with his servant. Thuroon watched him throw himself about recklessly. He wasn't sure if he should stop him from another night of destroying his own house—if he didn't, he was sure he would be taking the blame for it the next day. He cleared his throat.

Sir, Thuroon said.

Alejo lifted his head and looked at him—his eyes were gone, looking like a mad dog from the streets, he was breathing hard. He stopped moving.

Clean this mess, Alejo said. You caused it.

Sir, Thuroon said. I was about to go home and see my family.

Without hesitation, Alejo spoke.

If you don't fix this room, he said, you won't have a home or a family.

He left the room, bumping into Thuroon as he passed by.

I'm going to bed, Alejo said. In the morning, finish cleaning the living room walls. You're not doing a very good job.

Thuroon took a deep breath and started to pick up the books and torn pages, vases and sculptures, tables and chairs. He didn't finish until night had passed, and it was just before early morning. Instead of going home after he was done, he went back to the living room to finish cleaning the base of the walls. He was on his last bit of energy, and by the time he finished, the sun was already rising. He wiped the sweat from his forehead and took a deep breath, closing his eyes for a moment before opening them again and going to the kitchen to prepare Alejo's breakfast.

Alcee and Sari continued to trek through the forest. The wind was thick—though the forest shielded them from some of it, the pathways through the trees and brushes had caused an increase in the wind's effect, forcing the pair to protect themselves from falling or swinging branches. They closed their eyes and pushed back against the wind, as they were being pushed in all directions, sometimes having to hold against the roots of nearby trees.

They stopped from time to time to rest, sleep, and eat the food given by Pablo, which reinforced Sari's passion for her terse friend. Their travels met many obstacles as they ran into various creatures of the forest—most notably, a wild boar and a bear. The boar was aggressive and protective; however, Alcee and Sari found a way to kill it using sharp ends of broken branches. In total, the boar was stabbed or pierced with 18 pieces of makeshift spears and daggers. This turned out to be helpful for the two as the boar had provided more than enough food for them for at least a few days.

However, the bear was not as easy to conquer. They were resting for the night when they heard the bear's growl. Whether it was the remains of the boar, the smell of their skin, or its random search for food, they had caught the bear's attention—it was in a state of rage and hunger. When Alcee and Sari opened their eyes and realized what was taking place, they fought the urge to run away or shout or scream in panic. They remained calm.

We need to stay low, Sari said. Motionless. And when it's not looking, let's clear the area.

Because of their experience with the wild boar, the pair had made spears, short knives, and other stabbing tools out of what they could find in their surroundings, and they gathered rocks and short thick branches to throw in case of another encounter. When they saw the bear look away, Alcee and Sari split ways and hid behind some trees, holding their weapons. As the bear's back was facing them, they threw everything they had at it—spears, pieces of wood, clumps of shrubs—everything they hurled either hit or pierced the bear, and when it turned around to face Sari and Alcee, they continued to throw anything and everything at it. Soon, they had nothing else to defend themselves with, though they had done some damage—the bear was struck several times in its eyes, making it confused.

They remained still, motionless, hoping the bear would lose interest being injured and somewhat blinded. It sniffed around with a low growl until it eventually ventured off into the woods in the opposite direction, leaving Alcee and Sari by themselves.

Gone, Sari said.

I thought we were done, Alcee said.

I wonder if it was a mother, Sari said. Protecting her own or trying to find food for its cubs.

Perhaps, Alcee said. Perhaps, she knew where we were coming from.

Perhaps, Sari said. It knew we meant no harm.

After their encounter with the bear, the pair gathered their belongings, leaving the remains of the wild boar behind for the bear. They walked throughout the night, both sensing that the end of the forest was near as they felt the winds becoming stronger.

It was such a beautiful animal, Sari said.

Grand, Alcee said. Eloquent.

Hopefully, Sari said, she will come back to find the boar for nourishment.

Our lives are not too different, Alcee noted.

They imagined the end of the forest, leading to the fields which would lead to the volcano in which Dormier existed.

To make sure she was safe, Vienna traveled up the bank of the volcano, where Dormier was situated, and made her way to the fields—the same acres of land where Lash Gorge Stratus and Cirrus Stratus were. She made her way to the woods to hide for the time being. The field was so large that she didn't encounter either of the two, although she noticed a figure in the far distance; she thought that it was just a random farmer or nomad or hunter. She went to a lesser known area of the forest, not too close to the river where travelers and fishermen would always frequent. She wanted to make sure that no one could see her.

Finding a clearing within the woods, Vienna settled down with all that she had: a box of rats and some stale bread she managed to find on the streets of Dormier before leaving town. Having much experience with the forest, she wasn't too concerned about survival, as survival was all she knew. She knew which berries to eat and she knew how to hunt—she learned this when she would venture out into the forest for food as a last resort when she and her mother couldn't find any nourishment on the streets.

She covered the dirt with large leaves to make some kind of blanket and she lay upon it with her stomach facing the canopy above. In the room where she had been kept, she had lost all sense of time and day, and being in the woods was quite refreshing to her as she breathed in nature and felt the wind cover her skin. She heard chirps, buzzes, and the shuffling of woodland creatures around her. Pulling out some of the stale bread, she broke some of it into pieces and fed it to the rats. Without thinking, she started to sing a song her mother used to sing to her when she was a child. With her eyes closed, she sang loudly and beautifully and the woods themselves seemingly stopped their activities just to listen to her sing. She was soon surrounded by various forest animals, all hypnotized by her voice.

Dimanche

Fridatte Charon Perdu—Cirrus Stratus's paternal grandmother—before her death at the river, lived a life full of kindness and gentility. She was one of the first people to help bridge the gap between the various classes in Dormier including the untouchables, whom she cared for deeply.

Some of the nobles disagreed with her viewpoints; however, she didn't change her ways as she knew how living a tough life could be. She knew that, if anything, all of the people of Dormier needed love and care, including the thugs and prostitutes of the town. She was never close-minded and was always willing to help those in need. Unlike a grand portion of those who were wealthy, she never judged others.

Very different in her demeanor and mentality as her son when he entered politics, Dimanche could have very well become a politician and just before her death, she had met with the Principlist Party, which was the opposing party of Lash Gorge Stratus later on in his life—it was the party she felt most comfortable with as they were always trying to find ways to help the poor. She had met with them in regards to becoming the first lady to lead a political system in the town of Dormier, if not, the known world.

She was getting full support from all kinds of organizations and people of Dormier, and according to statisticians and various political experts, she would have won if she hadn't died during her visit to the river.

That fact that she died, one political member said, would have further ensured her victory.

Dimanche was well spoken, and she constantly read and studied, trying to gather as much knowledge as possible. Her curiosity and fascination for history, poetry, math, science, and literature was unending.

One evening, she and Leaus Perdu III sat in the study, reading children's stories to each other. It was well past her son's bedtime, but he was nowhere near sleep as his eyes remained large while Dimanche read adventure after adventure to him.

His favorite tale was about a cub who had lost his parents, and he was trying to find a way to survive in the wilderness on his own. It was the first story that made Leaus Perdu III realize the actual feeling of sadness as he would cry every time he heard the story of Little Cub, and every time they read it, he would ask his mother questions.

Mother, he said. Will he live?

Let's find out, Dimanche said.

Mother, he said. It's too sad that he lost his parents.

It is, child, she said. Let's find out what happens.

Leaus Perdu III would burst into sobs throughout the story hoping that the starving cub would find his parents or be able to live through the struggles of the wilderness on his own. His mother would rub his back, consoling him, but she never told him that it would be okay or that the cub lives. She always just said, let's see what happens, and by the end of the story, Leaus Perdu III's tears dried up, turning into laughter and smiles, after realizing that Little Cub will be able to survive with the help of his forest friends.

It's such a nice tale, Leaus Perdu III said. But next time, I hope it won't be the same.

Dimanche laughed at her son's imagination and his hope that the story, no matter how many times he read it or heard it, would be different the next time he read it.

It was this moment Lash Gorge Stratus thought about as he was on his hands and knees—his eyes facing the dirt. He grunted and coughed.

Little Cub, he said. Mother.

He tried to stand again but his attempt was unsuccessful as he fell back down on his hands and knees. His mind was full of images not of the present or future, but of the past. His mother, the one person to whom he connected the most—images of her flickered in his mind. It was the only medium he could use to connect to reality as he tried hard to fight his delirium.

He was in the river, just outside the volcano, swimming and playing—it was just him and his mother, as Leaus Perdu II was away dealing with the construction of a new opera house. They were both naked as Dimanche lay under the sun and Leaus Perdu III splashed around in the river. He had just learned how to swim not too long before, and he loved the new sensation of freedom while being in the currents as it pushed him in any direction—the force of nature was embedded within his body.

The feeling of splashed water, the river bed and its particles under his feet, and the fish swimming around him—it was a world new to him and he couldn't have enough of it.

Mother, he said. Come play.

In a bit, Dimanche said, sweet child.

She lay on the banks, letting the sun cover her skin, soporific and soothing.

Come mother, Leaus Perdu III said.

Dimanche stood up, smiling—her long black hair came down to the middle of her back. She ran her hands through her hair, letting her pores feel the sun.

Dimanche was naturally beautiful—never using any paint or powder to cover her face, the natural color of her skin beamed toward anyone in sight. She had several suitors. Whether bachelors or married men, she never was close to being tempted as all of her love was directed toward only two people—her son and her husband.

As Dimanche made her way down to the river from its bank, she saw a log drifting with the current. She shouted her son's name but there wasn't enough time for him to react as the log hit him in the back of the neck, causing his head to whip backward—knocking him out. Dimanche ran into the river and swam toward Leaus Perdu III, placing her arms underneath his body and lifting him above her head. She waded back to the banks using only the strength of her legs.

Once upon land, she ran her hands through his hair and whispered his name over and over. She elevated his head, resting it on a root and caressed his face with her knuckles, continuing to repeat his name.

Come back, she said. Come back to me, Leaus Perdu III.

He coughed and opened his eyes, his arms flailing about as he shouted for his mother.

I'm here, she said. And you were gone.

He started to cry, clinging to his mother's neck.

What did you see? she asked. What was in that world when your eyes were closed?

Lash Gorge Stratus's eyes were closed, breathing hard, still on his hands and knees.

I saw a world full of clouds—massive clouds, beaming with light, Lash Gorge Stratus said. I saw a kite drifting, weaving in out of the billows, and there was a child, jumping from one cloud to another.

He coughed and spat, specks of blood hit the dirt.

I saw you, he said. Carving a tree. And I saw father making syrup for morning waffles. I saw a lady, a stranger who was singing to me, and then I woke up.

Lash Gorge Stratus let go of his strength, his body falling down from his hands and knees to the dirt. His stomach pressed hard against the land—his head kissing the earth with bloodied spit.

When Vienna was young, growing up on the streets, she constantly observed the way her mother carried herself. She didn't know about her mother's past profession of prostitution and seduction at the time, and she always viewed Sari as someone of grace. Even when she did find out about her past, it didn't change her admiration for her mother—if anything, it grew.

Sari was a caring mother, always looking after her daughter's well-being, making sure she lived as comfortably as possible given their living situation.

As Vienna lay there in the middle of the woods with her box of rats, she thought about one particular night she had with her mother later on in life—she realized how important that moment was, and how her mother was such a gentle being.

During a rough winter night, full of winds and hail and sheets of rain, Vienna remembered being bundled up in shreds of blankets and torn cloths, sitting in the corner of the hut as the door made from a rug flew up and down, watching the weather outside exhibit its rage. She had been by herself all day and night as her mother was searching for food, more blankets and anything else that could help them face the tough winter days.

After a long day away, Vienna remembered seeing her mother walk through the rug door, drenched and shivering. She held a bundle in her hand made of cloth. She remembered seeing her in the worst conditions, her face chopped and worn as she walked inside, but as soon as she saw her daughter, Vienna saw her forlorn demeanor immediately switch to one full of love and comfort. Sari forced herself to stop shivering, masking it by constantly moving around and her grimace—she made it into a smile. Her face eased up, the dark shadows of her crevices on her face disappeared and softened quickly.

I love you Vienna, Sari said.

I love you mother, Vienna said. Are you warm?

My love, she said. Yes, I am. Now that I'm at home with you. And I have food for you.

Both Sari and Vienna hadn't eaten in three days. Vienna was starving, but she never said any word about it, nor revealed her hunger through any physical expression; she knew that food was scarce and she was old enough to realize the struggles of their living situation. Sari was also starving and she never showed it either, knowing that her weakness would filter into her daughter's mentality. She never let her daughter see her vulnerable or desperate.

She unwrapped a piece of cloth and revealed three pieces of bread—they were hardened and stale, but it was the first bit of nourishment they had seen in a few days.

Please, Sari said. Eat it all. You haven't had any food in quite some time. My apologies.

But Mother, Vienna said. Neither have you.

Sari smiled and sighed.

But I'm not even hungry, she said. Come, eat.

She gave her the pieces of bread. Vienna took it and looked at it, running her hands around its rough surface. She placed it on her lap and broke one piece into smaller pieces, not touching the remaining two larger pieces of bread. She gave her mother three of the smaller pieces and kept one of the smaller pieces for herself.

Take Mother, she said. Let's share and save the remaining pieces of bread for tomorrow.

Sari was almost in tears, but she did her best to keep her eyes dry. She always told herself that she would never let her daughter see her cry. She took two pieces and gave the other piece back to her daughter.

Let's keep it equal, she said.

Without another word said, they sat on the floor chewing their hardest to make sure their teeth cut through the hardened, stale bread.

Delicious, Vienna said.

I think it needs more cheese, Sari said.

They both laughed and continued to eat—continued to survive. The rug door was flickering up and down amidst the storm. Sari gave her daughter the last of the water, not letting her know that they didn't have any more left, though her own mouth was parched and craving water.

Drink, she said. It will soften the bread in your mouth.

What about you? Vienna said.

My pores have sucked in enough rainwater, Sari said. I'm good for another month.

She listened to Vienna take a sip of the water and smiled. It brought Sari happiness to know that Vienna would have at least some kind of food and water for the night. However, Vienna only took one sip before handing it back to her mother.

I will not drink anymore, she said. Until you have some.

Sari took a deep breath. She looked at her daughter with admiration—she was at a loss with how much she loved her daughter. It gave her some sense of satisfaction to know that her daughter exhibited a demeanor of giving and thoughtfulness. However, at the same time, she wished her daughter would consume all that she gave her instead of trying to share it.

Sari took the jug from Vienna and smiled.

You're too sweet, Sari said. Thank you, my dear.

She pretended to take a sip, faking a slurping noise and gave the jug back to Vienna, who also pretended to take a sip before giving it back to her mother.

We'll save the rest for tomorrow, Sari said.

The storm outside was getting louder, and the rug door nearly flew off.

Let me do something about this, Sari said.

She was tired, weak, and worn, but she knew she must carry on to make sure Vienna was as comfortable and safe as possible. She took some strips of wood and some nails and a hammer and walked outside.

Stay here, she said. I'll be right back.

Vienna remembered hearing the sounds of her mother hammering outside, a pounding that meshed into the crashes of thunder. She walked back inside, breathing hard and drenched. She was trying her best to stop shivering, but the cold had settled into her body too much to hide it—her teeth clattered.

Vienna managed to unwrap herself from the bundles of cloths that were tightly enveloped around her body. She took a longer piece of cloth and dried off her mother—her hair and body. She took another piece of cloth and wrapped it around her and hugged her, standing on her toes so that she could press her cheeks against her mother's face to give her some body heat. Sari hugged her back as Vienna rubbed her hands across her back and then she put her fingertips on the temples of her forehead and massaged it to help ease Sari's tension caused from the cold. Sari closed her eyes and for once in her life, she let her daughter take care of her.

Cirrus

Stratus made it back to Dormier. He was in disarray—he didn't know what to do upon his return. He had so many dreams and thoughts since the day of his exile, but now that he was back in Dormier, he was at a loss. He thought about going to his mother's hut, knowing that Alcee wouldn't be there, and that his home was most likely destroyed. He thought about finding Vienna or facing Alejo. He wondered whether he should give his apologies to all those living, to everyone whom he had caused trouble, as there were so many people he needed to find peace with.

He was back in the city he called home—but it was all a maze to him. The first action he took was to find a deserted alley to gather his thoughts and to take rest. He became overwhelmed with nostalgia; he had felt like it had been an infinite amount of time since he had been back at home.

He instinctively wanted to break into homes and businesses to make sure he and his mother could survive, as he had done every other day. He wanted to walk along the streets of the untouchables to say hi to those he cared for and to those who cared for him and his mother—he wanted to look after them to make sure they could make it until at least the next day.

In the alley, he spat and leaned his head against the side of a building made of concrete—an action he had done so many times before as this particular spot was a place in which he would find refuge when he needed to escape from the world. It was the one place that no one else in Dormier would frequent—whether or not they knew it existed, it was a lost soul of Dormier. It was Dormier in its darkest state at all times, and it was the only place Cirrus Stratus felt safe when he had to hide or escape.

The town was quiet the night he returned—its inhabitants were still in terror of being ransacked by Alejo and his crew who were in search for Lash Gorge Stratus. He closed his eyes and listened to the sounds that remained on a late abandoned Dormier night—sporadic pedestrians who had nothing to worry about—they had connections with Lash Gorge Stratus, and there was the howling of the street dogs and fighting cats.

Cirrus Stratus examined the alley and the bumps along the street—the buildings that formed the alley were deserted and broken. What was once a thriving area, full of markets and saloons, had faded away into a ghost street as the place had become too dangerous from politics and thugs. Even the untouchables stayed away, knowing that they would be putting themselves in danger. However, it was the place where Cirrus Stratus felt at home—comforted and relaxed. He didn't feel comfortable walking back to the street where his hut was situated along with the other untouchables— he wanted to hide more than anything else, or rather, he didn't want anyone to know that he was back. He wasn't sure about the state of Dormier, and how his return would affect the town, or Alejo, Vienna, his mother or anyone else.

He realized his own hunger for food, as it had been quite a time since he had last eaten. He stood up, stretched, and yawned.

Bread, he thought.

He walked out of the alley in search of food—nothing was open, but he went to the trash can of one particular restaurant and found some bread and meatballs. Without hesitation, he took it out and started to eat, proud of himself for not breaking into any restaurant or house to steal food. The nourishment he found was not old, as it had been thrown away earlier that day, and he savored every bite as if he was at the fancy eatery where he and his mother and father used to eat when he was a child.

Lash

Gorge Stratus found himself standing up. He was stumbling, but he was standing up for the first time in two days.

Berries, he said. Dormier.

Drenched in cold sweat, he unbuttoned his shirt and took it off, using it to dry his forehead and hair. The sun was at its peak, and he squinted into the sky to see large winged birds gliding and swooping in the air, appearing to slow down time. The wind shifted direction, blowing against his face.

Condors, he noticed.

Still squinting, he saw one flying directly ahead, toward him.

No, Lash Gorge Stratus said.

It came closer and closer. Lash Gorge Stratus stayed still, in disbelief that the condor was actually going after him. He could see its beak getting closer. He imagined himself with Cirrus Stratus, standing on the edge of the volcano, watching the condors twirling around them.

It looks like they're swimming, Cirrus Stratus said.

Leaus Perdu III was holding his hand.

It looks like they're sliding on ice, Leaus Perdu III said The sky is under their control.

It was a memory that flashed in his mind right before he saw the condor directly in front of him. It pecked at his chest before flying back up into the naked sky. Lash Gorge Stratus's chest was bleeding—that one peck made a gash in the right side of his chest. He didn't say a word, nor did he yelp in pain. He remained standing, as his senses were becoming more honed into reality after days of being disillusioned. Still holding his shirt, he covered the deep cut with it while looking at the same condor making another loop. He didn't run or move—he stood still.

Ice, he said.

He spat.

Swimming, he added.

He saw its beak right before it pecked the top of his head, causing him to stumble back. He felt the skin split and the blood coming out, soaking his hair. He took off his slacks and tore them into pieces, taking one large shred of the cloth to wrap it around his head. He gritted his teeth as he saw the condor making another loop.

I'm no rabbit, Lash Gorge Stratus said.

He watched it come toward him, tapping his foot against the grass, counting each beat.

Come on, he said.

The condor steadily approached as Lash Gorge Stratus still had his eyes squinted.

Come on now, he said.

He closed his hands to make fists. His eyes flashed wide open as he dodged to the right, swinging his right fist, hitting the condor in the head, causing it to squawk. The large bird fluttered onto the ground before gathering its senses and flew back up into the sky.

Lash Gorge Stratus was breathing hard—his hands were still in fists, his posture still bent in the position to defend himself. He grunted.

What are you going to do now, he said.

The condor was making another loop in the air, but this time, as it flew toward Lash Gorge Stratus's direction, it remained high in the sky. It flew over him and continued to soar as Lash Gorge Stratus watched it fade away into a tiny speck in the sky.

I'm no rabbit, he said. Can't get me.

He turned around and looked ahead to see the outline of the volcano. He sighed and started to walk, thinking to himself that he must get home to get the city back under his order and to finish off what he started with Alcee, Cirrus Stratus, Sari, and her daughter.

Let this end, he said. Whether I live or die, let this all end.

To keep his mind occupied, he used his memories to let the time pass, but the memories were not of his time as a politician and leader of the Ethicginian Party. It wasn't about his growth as a man full of hate, greed, and power—he pushed his memories back further to a certain time he had with Cirrus Stratus.

Where are we going? Cirrus Stratus had asked.

He was holding his father's hand.

You'll see, Leaus Perdu III said. Be patient.

Where's mother? Cirrus Stratus asked.

Without losing his stride, and without hesitation, he thought about Alcee, who had remained at home to prepare for their son's birthday. Leaus Perdu III, himself, was struggling not to reveal the surprise to his son. However, he remained calm as they walked to their destination.

She's working, Leaus Perdu III said.

Where are we going? Cirrus Stratus asked again.

We're almost there, he said. You're growing up, son.

Cirrus Stratus jumped up and down, remembering that it was his birthday.

They reached their destination—it was a hidden part of the volcano, where mining had taken place years ago as the city was just beginning to develop, but after a massive cave-in that killed everyone inside, the city deserted the place, especially because nothing valuable was ever found. It had become a forgotten place. However, Leaus Perdu III never stopped going there. He would secretly visit the area by himself and with a small chisel, he would tap away amidst the rubble—it wasn't so much for the need to find riches, as they were already a prominent family, but it was more for the sense of discovery—the adventure was finding what others couldn't.

He found all kinds of gems, including sapphire, emeralds, rubies, and diamonds. He never took them—he just kept them there and smiled every time he found one—this was his pleasure.

Where are we? Cirrus Stratus said.

We are in a secret place, Leaus Perdu III said.

He pulled a small hammer out from his pocket and gave it to his son.

Tap on the walls, he said.

His son squinted his eyes and looked around the cave before asking why.

For discovery, he said.

Cirrus Stratus took the hammer and started to knock

against the wall, bits and pieces fell down—the movement in itself made him curious and excited. After one strong tap, a huge chunk fell, revealing a large gem—a sapphire.

Once he saw it, he stopped tapping and looked at his father in silence. Leaus Perdu III remained silent, smiling. Cirrus Stratus looked at the gem, sticking out his hand.

It's outstanding, he said. Can I touch it?

Of course, his father said. You found it. Take it out. It's yours.

He rubbed his fingertips against the surface of the gem before digging them into the wall and pulling the sapphire out. He held in both of his palms. He tried to give it to his father, but he didn't make any movement to take it.

It's yours, he said.

Cirrus Stratus looked up at and stared into the ceiling of the cave. He put it between his teeth and pressed down on it before taking it back out.

It's pretty solid, he said.

He tossed it up and down, thinking of what he should do with it. With a large smile, he looked at his father.

For my birthday, he said, I would like to present this to my mother.

Leaus Perdu III put his hand on his son's shoulder.

Such a lovely thought, he said. Your kindness and generosity are well respected. Much can be learned from you, by many, including myself.

Cirrus Stratus continued to play with the gem until he had a realization—he stopped tossing it up and down.

Father, he said. What is it?

It's a jewel, Leaus Perdu III explained. Like in those adventure stories where you read about the characters searching for treasure. This particular jewel is called a sapphire.

Mother deserves this treasure, Cirrus Stratus said.

She will love it, Leaus Perdu III had said. Come, let's go back home to surprise her.

Surprise, Lash Gorge Stratus thought now.

He continued to walk toward the volcano, somehow managing to channel his strength, walking with great force. The sky was clear of condors—the clouds were still gone. The sun was on its way down, as Lash Gorge Stratus used his own shadow to gauge the passing of time. He went back to his memory.

They were back at home—Alcee had finished preparing dinner, and the house was beginning to fill with guests—friends of Leaus Perdu III and Alcee, and their children who were close to Cirrus Stratus. There was a small orchestra playing their favorite songs. They danced nonstop—Alcee and Leaus Perdu III, as always, caught everyone's attention, causing the crowd to stop dancing and watch in awe as the couple twirled around the room in harmony. It was as if nothing else around them existed—just them and the music in their heads. There was the world, and then there was them.

Even when the orchestra took a break to transition from one song to the next, they continued to dance as if the music never stopped playing. If it wasn't for Cirrus Stratus, the two would have danced for the rest of the night and well into the next morning as they had done before on numerous occasions. Cirrus Stratus, dressed in a waist coat and tie—his hair slicked and neatly parted, and his black shoes, polished and beaming, was having a great time playing with his friends and engaging in conversations with the adults about literature, history, and philosophy. He charmed them all.

At some point during Leaus Perdu III and Alcee's entertaining dance, Cirrus Stratus ran up to them and took his parents' hands, and started to dance with them.

Dance, Leaus Perdu III said. Dance, dance, dance. Let the music of the world into the music of your soul.

My son, Alcee said. My dancing gem.

Cirrus Stratus put his hand in his pocket and pulled out the sapphire wrapped in a small piece of cloth and tied with strands from a horse's tail.

My son, Alcee said. What is this?

It's for you, Cirrus Stratus said. Father and I found it earlier today.

She kissed her son on the cheek.

This was his idea, too, Leaus Perdu III said. He found it and wanted to give it to you for his birthday celebration.

Alcee, having not opened the gift yet, began to tear up. She gently took it from his hands and slowly unwrapped it as Leaus Perdu III and Cirrus Stratus watched—the son bursting with anticipation and excitement. She unwrapped it. Her eyes became large, still watery.

So pretty, she said.

It reminds me of you, Cirrus Stratus said.

Alcee bent down and kissed him on the cheek again.

Thank you, she said. Such a gentleman. My son—your kindness and love know no boundaries.

Leaus Perdu III kissed his son on the top of his head.

What will you do with it? Cirrus Stratus asked.

I will turn it into a necklace, she said. And forever keep it close to me.

They all continued to dance well into the night. Cirrus Stratus was awake until the last guest left.

Gem, Lash Gorge Stratus said. Family.

He continued to walk toward the volcano, not stopping to rest as he was determined to get back to Dormier. His eyes were weak though—holding back any kind of sentiment, he kept his eyes wide open so as to not let them droop.

One day, he thought, I will sleep forever. But not today or tomorrow. Not until all is in control again.

Vienna slept for two days without waking up. Her body needed rest and her mind needed to slow down, though she was constantly dreaming about the unknown physical appearance of Cirrus Stratus, the two horses that were killed for her, her mother, and her time in the basement of Lash Gorge Stratus's headquarters.

The rats slept for the two days as well. Loyal to their caretaker, they remained in the box, though Vienna had left it open in case they wanted to leave. Vienna had named each of the four rats based on their various physical characteristics. Cheval was the name for the one who had a string of puffy hair going from the head down to the back of its neck; Deer hopped more than he walked; Javier liked to walk backward; and Nelia Amelia was the only female of the group. The rats enjoyed her care to the point that they responded to their names respectively when called upon by Vienna.

When Vienna woke up, naked and calm, her first action was to see if the rats were still there. She sighed as she saw all of four of them still in the container.

Hi, she said. How are you doing, Javier, Cheval, Deer, and Nelia Amelia? It's quite a day.

The rats moved around in excitement, upon hearing her voice.

I'm not sure how long I slept, she said. But I needed it.

She rubbed her belly as she listened to a redbird chirping from a nearby branch.

By any chance, Vienna said. Would you all know Cirrus Stratus?

The rats scuffled about in the container, making their own chirping noises.

If so, she said. Please tell me about him. I'm so curious. He has caused such a frenzy over me, and I don't even know him.

Vienna closed her eyes and heard the rats talk in unison.

He will be your husband one day, the rats said. You two will be the greatest lovers of Dormier. You two will lead the town back into harmony.

The rats scurried around as Vienna opened her eyes and smiled.

Thank you, she said. You are such mysteries.

She stood up for the first time since she had gone into the woods to sleep. She bent backwards, raising her arms, stretching stomach and thighs. She picked up her box of rats and her gown, but she didn't put it on and started to walk back to Dormier.

Sari and Alcee were back in Dormier—they arrived just after morning, and as they walked through the cave of the volcano, they could hear the familiar sounds of the city, causing their skin to rise, as a culmination of emotions gathered in their heads.

When they exited the cave that opened up to the city before them, their reality was in much disarray—the day was surreal to them. In the tint of light, the people, the noises, they were all magical to them. It felt both foreign and cozy—both strange and comfortable.

As they walked through the town, people looked at them as if they were brought back from the dead—with wide eyes and opened mouths, they were in awe.

Ghosts, one person said.

Weren't they dead? another person asked.

By the hands of Lash Gorge Stratus, I thought, said another onlooker.

A child ran up to them and tugged on Sari's cloth.

Good Miss, he said, good Miss.

Sari looked down and smiled.

Yes, she said. Good sir.

Are you alive? he asked.

I would hope so, Sari said.

We all thought you were dead, he said.

Maybe we were, she said. Maybe we still are.

The child scrunched his shoulders.

What if we all are really dead, he said, and we are just living in someone else's dream?

But whose dream? Sari asked.

The child looked up into the sky, losing himself in the moving clouds.

Maybe in the dream of my little sister—the one I never met. She died upon birth.

He hugged Sari's leg and ran off.

Sweet child, Alcee said.

What if, Sari said. What if.

As they walked through the town, not really knowing where they should go, and as everyone stared at them, they lost themselves in a conversation about dreams and reality sparked by the child, until they found themselves on the street where their huts once existed.

They recognized a few people, and a few people recognized them, but many huts had been destroyed or deserted—both Sari's and Alcee's huts were ransacked, just as they had expected.

Time to start again, Sari said.

Perhaps it's for the best, Alcee said.

Should we wait? Sari asked. As soon as they hear that we're back, I'm sure they'll return.

Much worse can happen if they find us again, Alcee said. Perhaps a kidnapping or a killing.

Most probably, Sari said.

They continued to walk along the street—the untouchables were much more cordial to them than those who saw the two walking through the market area of the town.

Jinesha, a neighbor of Sari, one who would often look after Vienna when she was a child while Sari searched for food, walked up to them—half-smiling, half in tears.

My gentle being, Jinesha said.

She hugged Sari and kissed her on each side of the cheek and on the forehead.

I've been too worried, she said.

Although they had never spoken to each other, both Alcee and Jinesha knew each other's faces. They hugged each other as if they knew each other since childhood.

Welcome home, Jinesha said.

The three stood there, and Sari and Alcee told her about their journey and Jinesha updated the two about the happenings of Dormier.

We were all so lost, Jinesha said.

But when were we ever found? Sari said.

This city, Jinesha said, even the untouchables feel an added pressure from the city. How could that be so? We've lost what we didn't have.

Upon seeing Jinesha talking to the two, another untouchable, Firia, walked up to Sari and Alcee, and with mutual recognition, they hugged each other and exchanged cordials.

Home, Firia said. Welcome. We are all alive, but this city has become dead.

Cirrus

Stratus was only a few blocks away from where Sari and the group were resting at Firia's place. They had walked past the alley—where Cirrus Stratus was sitting —it was an alley that no one looks at when passing. They didn't notice him, and he didn't see them either as his head was still leaning back against the wall of a building, his eyes closed, trying to gather his plans on turning Dormier back to a place of no fear.

As the group walked by the alley, Cirrus Stratus heard voices, including the voice of his mother; however, he thought that they were just in his head. He was still in a somewhat surreal state—tired and hungry and recovering from the place that didn't exist. The real world, the world he once knew, felt foreign to him.

When he opened his eyes, he felt the morning—he felt the past, the past when mornings were his family and they were in the acres of their land, having breakfast in the field, or running around and playing some kind of game with his family. He saw himself lying in the field, with his parents, with their faces up to the sky in silence.

Mother, Cirrus Stratus said. Father. What happened?

He arched his back to stretch before standing up.

Thuroon

Thuroon had been working all day at Alejo's mansion, yet he hadn't seen Alejo at all while he was performing his duties. He had made Alejo lunch per a request he had made the day before—carrots, potatoes, lamb, and lentils—but when he saw that his dish was still at the dinner table, untouched, he went upstairs to find him as dinner time was approaching.

Alejo was sitting in the corner of his bedroom, barefoot and shirtless. He was on the floor, his head planted in his hands, with his elbows resting on his raised knees. Thuroon noticed the scratches all over his body and arms.

Sir, Thuroon said. Sir.

Alejo moaned.

Sir, Thuroon said. Do you need help?

Alejo ran his fingers through his hair, still keeping his head down. Thuroon could hear quiet sniffles. He walked in a bit closer to him.

Sir, he said. Would you like some dinner?

Alejo spat on the floor, still not looking up. Thuroon took his rag and bent down to wipe it. Alejo started to cackle, startling Thuroon. His cackling turned into a cough as he lifted his head. His eyes were dark, red, watery with tears coming down from his deep coughs. His spasms subsided.

Sir, Thuroon said.

Alejo stared at him—his eyes small, squinting—he looked lost to Thuroon. He couldn't tell if he was staring at him, through him, or past him.

Alejo's voice was low and raspy.

What do you think of me? he said.

His eyes became large and round, half-smiling—he growled.

Thuroon saw the scratches on his face.

Sir, Thuroon said. You are an honest man. I admire your ability to always be yourself.

Why are you still here? Alejo asked him.

Sir, Thuroon said.

Why do you still work for me? he asked. I may be honest but that doesn't mean I'm kind or good or loving.

Sir, Thuroon said, to be honest, I've stayed because I have a family, and I can support them well by working for you.

Alejo responded quickly, half-laughing.

I must be paying you too much, he said.

Thuroon couldn't help but to laugh. It was the first time Alejo had ever joked with Thuroon.

But that says nothing about me, Alejo said. Only that I'm wealthy.

Your wealth is kind, Thuroon said.

Alejo laughed until he started to cough again. Heaving deeply, he caught his breath and continued to laugh.

Sir, Thuroon said. Would you like to come down for dinner?

Thuroon, Alejo began.

Thuroon couldn't remember the last time he had called him by name, at least in a gentle way.

You can make hay taste exquisite, Alejo said. Whatever you cook, I will eat with great infatuation.

Sir, Thuroon said. Yes. I will start my preparation.

And I will make myself presentable, Alejo said.

Thuroon was quite taken aback with the way Alejo was acting. It was the most he had ever been cordial to Thuroon, and it confused him. It made him happy, too, to know that Alejo could show an emotion other than rage and arrogance. Even though Alejo wasn't outwardly kind, it made Thuroon want to stay, to help him become more like the man he thought Alejo could be.

Alejo washed himself as Thuroon prepared dinner. Alejo refused to look in the mirror. He wore his best clothes, dressed in a suit and tie, clean shaven with his hair neatly parted. He sighed before walking downstairs to the dinner room where he saw an exquisite meal of mashed potatoes, green peas, a steak covered in cheese, and a bed of oysters. Thuroon stood in the corner waiting for him.

Alejo sat down at the table—his being, Thuroon noticed, was full of light. The energy that Alejo emitted was welcoming. When he spoke, his tone was of that Thuroon had never heard before—it was pleasant and soft; it was new. He saw him smile—a smile Alejo had never given while Thuroon had been working for him.

Please, Thuroon said. Enjoy.

This looks amazing, Alejo said. Come. Sit and eat with me.

Sir, Thuroon said. Thank you. But I prepared only enough for you.

Without hesitation, Alejo took his salad plate and emptied it onto his dinner plate. He started to take some of his food and put it on the salad plate. He placed it in the open spot directly in front of him.

Here, Alejo said. Sit. Please. Join me.

Sir, Thuroon said.

Please do, Alejo said.

Thuroon sat across from him. Alejo handed him a spare fork and knife and they began to eat.

So delicious, Alejo said. You're quite a chef. My favorite in town.

This was the first time Thuroon had ever sat down with Alejo—it was also the first time he had ever seen Alejo eating with someone at the dinner table. He was nervous.

Sir, Thuroon said. This is greatly appreciated.

Much deserved, Alejo said.

Thuroon bowed his head for a short time before starting to eat.

Where are my manners? Alejo said. Let me get you something to drink. How about a glass of wine?

Thuroon didn't know how to respond—wide eyes and raised eyebrows, he looked at Alejo, who started to laugh.

I'll be right back, Alejo said.

He stood and walked to the cabinet and poured a glass of wine.

Here, he said. Have a sip. It's soft and soothing.

Wonderful, Thuroon said.

He couldn't remember if he ever had such an expensive, elegant glass of wine before.

How is your family? Alejo asked.

Again, Thuroon didn't know how to respond. The situation felt strange to him, but he kept with it, not knowing how long this would last. He started to talk about his family, and the more he talked about his children and wife, the more Alejo's eyes gleamed—they became watery at times as Thuroon continued to talk about his life at home.

Your love for them, Alejo said, it's amazing—full of great energy.

He took another bite of his steak and sighed.

I was kind once, Alejo said.

Yes sir, Thuroon said.

This meal is so delicious, Alejo said. I would like to present it to a museum to keep the memory of such great nourishment.

Sir, Thuroon said. I am humbled.

I will be leaving soon, Alejo said. Taking a trip. I take it that you can look after this place.

Of course, Thuroon said. I will treat it like it's my own place.

Then it's in good care, Alejo said.

He finished his last bite of his steak and looked at Thuroon with watery eyes. He took his glass of wine and lifted it up. Thuroon did the same, lifting his glass of wine.

To the wonderful, humble, and the loving, Alejo said. To the giving.

They touched glasses and took the last sips of their wine. Alejo took a deep breath and sighed.

I will be going on a journey, Alejo said. For quite some time. It will be quite an adventure.

Sir, Thuroon said.

This place has basically become your place, Alejo said.

How long will you be gone? Thuroon asked.

I don't know, he said. But it will be quite a journey.

Though Cirrus Stratus was walking, not realizing where he was going, he was making his way to a place that had such a great memory for him. He found himself at the cave, where his father once took him on his birthday—the day he found the gem that he eventually gave to his mother.

He stood in the cave and moved his head in full motion, in circles, bringing him back to that time with Leaus Perdu III.

He knocked on the walls—dirt and dust and rock falling to the ground, but there was no gem like the last time, when he had gone years ago. He traced his fingers along the rock walls, pieces falling here and there. He looked deep into the holes of the wall and found himself in a world full of the past—alongside his father, holding a gem, a memory he could not normally remember easily. It was a hidden memory—a night of dancing, his mother's kiss, his father's smile. He left his fingerprints on the walls upon remembering his birthday. His mother and father freshly ingrained in his thoughts, he lowered his head and closed his eyes.

Where are we? he said. Where is our world? What happened? Where are you?

Sari and Alcee were standing in the middle of the rubble that once was Sari's hut. Firia had given them some spare material to help them rebuild their homes, including thick rugs to be used for doors, bamboo to provide structure as well two broken chairs that were still usable.

Where should we begin? Sari asked.

I say we start with the bamboo, Alcee said.

They started to build the outside, using rope and rags to keep the bamboo together, and in between the gaps, large rocks were used to fill the space. They worked efficiently, finishing the outside before the day's end. And throughout the night they worked on setting up the inside as much as possible, using candles as light.

It actually looks better than before, Sari said.

It looks great, Alcee said. A new beginning.

Now, Sari said, let's set you up.

They went to Alcee's place, which was in the same rubble state as Sari's—without hesitation, they started to work on getting the place fixed, and by morning's time, Alcee had a new home.

So surreal, Alcee said. My new home.

The sun was coming up and the sounds of the songbirds began to make their way throughout the town.

I don't know what to do now, Sari said.

Sleep, Alcee said.

Sari agreed and went back to her place to rest. Alcee did the same. Though neither could actually sleep, they were able to get some rest.

Alcee thought about her son. Sari thought about her daughter. The air was hot and damp as they lay turning from side to side on their dirt beds full of bumps.

When they met later on in the morning, they both noticed the other looking distraught.

You didn't sleep, Sari said.

Neither did you, Alcee said.

They hugged and went off to walk the streets together to find food for the day; if not for the day, at least for the morning.

They failed at the markets, and they couldn't find any nourishment in the bins on the streets or anywhere else.

We must keep our spirits, Sari said.

We have no reason to starve, Alcee said. Our souls are full of love and hope.

They walked around, asking anyone they saw about Vienna and Cirrus Stratus. Some answered, some didn't. Some spoke, some walked away without saying a word.

Do you want me dead? one man said. What kind of question is that, to ask in these days full of fear and death?

Another stranger just nodded his head and walked away.

I've heard of them, one lady said. I thought they were dead.

Another lady pretended she didn't understand them and walked off shaking her head.

One man's eyes, upon hearing their names, became large and wide. He scratched his head and looked around.

Oh yes, he said. I've heard of him and her, Cirrus Stratus and Vienna.

He smiled.

They are the future of Dormier. And the future will arrive.

What do you mean? Sari said.

I mean, he said. Dormier will explode and sleep and all will be well.

And who are you? Alcee said. What is your name? And have you seen them recently?

The man, bald headed, rubbed his protruding stomach.

I said all that you need to know, he replied. And all that you need to know, you will know.

We need more, Sari said.

It will be fun, the man said.

He laughed and walked away as Sari and Alcee looked at him until he disappeared.

What did he mean? Alcee asked.

What he said, Sari answered, is the only hope we have heard of so far. I suspect they're still alive.

I will never think otherwise, Alcee said, until I, myself, am dead.

For we live now because they are alive, Sari said.

They looked into the distance—the sky was blue and clear— and they saw a bird in the distance, but they couldn't tell which kind.

It soars, Alcee said.

Holding hands, they continued to walk the streets in search of their children and food.

Lash

Gorge Stratus was nearing the volcano, but he didn't want to enter the city of Dormier the common way; he wanted to keep his presence to a minimum. Instead, he went into the city using the alternate, lesser known route—through the cave, the one he had taken his son to on his birthday.

He guided himself through the small hole, making it bigger as he propelled his body to drill his way forward, widening the walls. He took deep breaths and held them so as to not inhale the dust and dirt that surrounded him.

He closed his eyes in the dark, and moved and moved until he reached an opening—he was able to stand and walk. Still dark, he used his hands and pushed against the walls to guide himself forward until he reached another opening which gave way to light.

Lash Gorge Stratus opened his eyes as he felt the heat upon his eyelids. At first, all was blurry, and as he blinked repeatedly, he was able to grasp reality. He was able to see before him, but he still used his hands, pushing them against the wall to help him go forward. The dirt would crumble, softly—reminding him of the day of the sapphire with Cirrus Stratus on his son's birthday.

Gentle, fallen, Lash Gorge Stratus said.

He stumbled as he walked, tired but still determined. He refused any result other than making it back to his home—his city.

Being able to catch a scent of the Dormier air, he took one of the pathways that looked familiar to him. He saw a figure sitting on the ground before him—the head leaning against the wall. Lash Gorge Stratus squinted.

Where are you? he said. Why are you here?

The body didn't move, nor did it acknowledge Lash Gorge Stratus's presence.

Speak, Lash Gorge Stratus said, or I will cross you, and if you attempt to attack, I will defend myself.

He shuffled his feet, still not hearing any response.

Are you dead? Lash Gorge Stratus asked. I will kill you.

The body still remained motionless. Lash Gorge Stratus squinted again, still trying to adjust to the light.

Reveal yourself, he shouted.

He began to think that the figure before him was either dead or drunk, though he knew of no one else who had ever ventured the cave since its demise apart from himself and his son. He proceeded forward to pass him, but with caution. He stared at the figure, as he walked by, and Lash Gorge Stratus was unable to see the person's face. He kept walking. Upon a few steps, he heard a voice.

Father, Cirrus Stratus said.

Lash Gorge Stratus stopped walking. His eyes gave into the bright light—he closed them. He recognized the voice immediately upon his son's calling.

Son, Lash Gorge Stratus said.

Father, Cirrus Stratus said. Where are you going?

Lash Gorge Stratus glided his feet over the rubble, back and forth, making a soft whirring sound.

Home, he said. My child.

Father, Cirrus Stratus said. Are you going to kill me?

I don't know, son.

Me neither, my father, Cirrus Stratus said.

What are you going to do? Lash Gorge Stratus asked.

He walked up to his son and stood directly in front of him and patted him on the head.

Where's mother? Cirrus Stratus asked.

She's dancing in my head, Lash Gorge Stratus said.

Where's mother? Cirrus Stratus repeated.

She's everywhere, Lash Gorge Stratus said.

Are you going to kill her?

I don't know, Lash Gorge Stratus said.

He bent down to kiss his son on the head but stopped halfway. He stood straight and rubbed his eyes. As he started to walk away, he looked back at his son.

Go home. I'll see you there.

I'll see you there father, Cirrus Stratus said.

Bye son, Lash Gorge Stratus replied.

He recognized his location, and knew how to exit the cave, which opened to a field that led straight to Dormier. He hesitated, at first, to leave the cave as he thought about Cirrus Stratus. He grunted.

I'll see him again, he said.

Back in the cave, Cirrus Stratus popped his head against the wall, eyes open, mouth open, he stared at the ceiling— weak and unstable, he was trying hard to get back to reality, not really knowing if he actually had a conversation with his father.

He stood up, dizzying himself.

Home, Cirrus Stratus said.

He started to stumble his way toward the opening of the cave.

Vienna made it to Dormier during the night. Full of energy, she walked through town, holding her box of rats and looking around for someone to talk to, but the streets were empty, as it was late at night.

She ran into the occasional homeless drunks but they were not too communicative, their grasp of reality being far gone. She would ask them questions, but to no avail except for one untouchable who was searching the richer areas in hope of more coins and food.

How are you doing? Vienna asked her.

The sky, she said.

The sky? Vienna repeated.

The sky will be black and puffed, she said.

How come? Vienna asked.

Because the dirt, because the concrete, because the rubble, she said. They let me know.

Thank you my dear, Vienna said.

The lady tapped her on the shoulder and walked off. Vienna was grateful to have a conversation with her, and though she couldn't quite understand what she was saying, it was the first human words spoken to her since she escaped from her kidnapping.

Dark and puffed, Vienna said.

Finding a hidden spot to rest, Vienna stopped and sat down to wait for the morning to come. She couldn't sleep so she talked to the rats for company until the sun rose to the songs of birds.

We are back home now, Vienna said.

In unison, the rats spoke.

Oh dear, they said.

Vienna laughed. Worried? she said.

Very much so, they said. We are most likely dead here.

You all and everyone else, Vienna said, including me.

All will happen, the rats said. We may be alive, we may be dead. But all will happen.

Fickle rats, Vienna said. Let's find food.

The sun was rising, and the morning songs began.

Breakfast, the rats said.

They hopped over each other and paced quickly, back and forth and in circles.

Vienna, with the box in her hand, left her resting place to enter into the awakening town, excited to see her town's people—she looked to converse with strangers.

She came up to one lady who was selling knitted hats decorated with small shiny objects—red, blues, yellows, and greens made up most of the colorful ornamentation. Vienna approached her, smiling, asking the lady how she was doing. The lady's face was full of crinkles—her hair was gray, and her eyes drooped over the darkness of the skin right underneath. She didn't smile; however, when she spoke, her voice was full of kindness and solace—it was soothing, reminding Vienna of the more generous times of her life as an untouchable with her mother, times of comfort and serenity before Lash Gorge Stratus had caused dread and fear throughout the city.

They look wonderful, Vienna said.

Thank you my dear, the lady said.

She looked at her customer carefully—her eyebrows, her hair, her chin and breasts.

I know you, she said, or I know about you.

Vienna looked into the sky, thinking.

And what is your name? Vienna asked.

The lady coughed.

I am Thockley, she said. Who are you my dear?

Vienna told the woman her own name and to this Thockley raised her eyebrows.

Yes, Thockley said. You are dead, from what I hear.

Oh my, Vienna said. I haven't heard that. Should I be dead? I'd be sorry to disappoint.

She laughed.

Now, now, Thockley said. Stop playing these games—are you dead or alive?

I'm afraid I'm alive, Vienna said.

This is good, Thockley said.

She put her hand on Vienna's shoulder—it wasn't until now that she realized that she was still naked, holding her gown in hand. She laughed and started to put on the ragged cloth.

I understand you want to cover yourself, Thockley said. However, I love that you didn't notice that you were naked—that you felt comfortable bare while amid this town.

It's my most comfortable state, Vienna said. However, I don't want to cause any more trouble or attention walking around without any clothes.

Your purity, Thockley said, your energy, full of love. So natural, it brings light to such a place that has been in much turmoil for the longest of times.

I've been disconnected, Vienna said, as you can see.

I see nothing but pure beauty, Thockley said. Clear and vivid. You must be the loveliest person here—not only physically, but spiritually, too.

Oh, I'm just an untouchable, Vienna said.

Very much so, Thockley said. You *are* untouchable.

The rats squeaked, seemingly listening to their conversation, perhaps agreeing with Thockley's compliments given to Vienna.

And who are these lovely creatures here? Thockley asked.

The beauty of Dormier, Vienna said. They are more so than what you say I am.

She introduced each rat to Thockley.

Do you know? Thockley said.

Vienna didn't know how to respond, looking at her new friend with a scrunched face.

Do you know? Thockley said.

I'm afraid I don't know, Vienna said.

Thockley smiled and put her hand on Vienna's shoulder again. The sounds of Dormier in the morning became vibrant to Vienna—making her feel at home again. She sighed.

You will save us, Thockley said. You and the one in your future will save us. I can feel it.

Oh my, Vienna said. Who is this other one you're talking about?

The one who flew kites, she said. The one who belongs in the clouds.

Her smile remained, but she took her hand off Vienna's shoulder to pat her on the back, while giving her a hug. She shook her head.

Thanks, Thockley said.

With nothing else said, she walked away laughing, leaving Vienna in a state of confusion. She could hear her laughing turning into whistling. Vienna's eyes looked up into the sky.

Cirrus Stratus, she said.

Before walking into the main part of town after leaving the cave where he met his estranged son, Lash Gorge Stratus wrapped himself in rags he found as he walked through the streets to keep himself incognito.

For the first time in years, since he was a bowler playing in the championships, he felt nervous. He kept his head down, his face half covered in shreds of cloths, and he felt the emptiness in his stomach as he entered Dormier. He couldn't remember the last time he walked around town without being feared.

As he entered town, he was met by a homeless man—a beggar who had been on the streets since he was a child. Lash Gorge Straus recognized him as he and Alcee would help him out from time to time, giving him money and food. His name was Yumi Malesca Couvreau, but Lash Gorge Stratus didn't show that he knew him. He felt somewhat embarrassed as he hadn't talked to him since he entered politics.

You look worse than me, Yumi Malesca Couvreau said.

Where am I? Lash Gorge Stratus said.

He wanted to come off as a drifter.

Yumi Malesca Couvreau smiled and nodded his head.

This is the volcano city, he said. Dormier. The sleeping town that was once full of magma.

Lash Gorge Stratus looked at him, not knowing what to say next.

You need food, Yuni Malesca Couvreau said. I will help you.

The softness in his voice made Lash Gorge Stratus

remember the days when life was different—when he had a family and life was full of love and giving.

Your eyes, Yumi Malesca Couvreau said. They speak of stories.

Nothing remarkable, Lash Gorge Stratus said. No stories worth telling.

Yumi Malesca Couvreau took Lash Gorge Stratus by the wrist.

Come, he said. Follow me.

He led the drifter down a few blocks and turned into an alley where there was a single hut made of bamboo, rocks, and rugs.

Not trying to reveal his identity, Lash Gorge Stratus spoke.

I've heard of the untouchables, he said. Is this the place where they live?

Are we that famous? Yumi Malesca Couvreau asked.

The homeless man shook his head.

But no, the homeless man continued, the untouchables are here in this town, but this isn't the street where they live. I once lived there but moved away.

Why? Lash Gorge Stratus asked, though he knew the answer.

Because, Yumi Malesca Couvreau said. The living situation was worsening, dangerous, even for us. Constantly being ransacked, beaten—I miss the days when we were just ignored.

Why such treachery? Lash Gorge Stratus said.

Again, he knew the answer.

Yumi Malesca Couvreau smiled. He put his hand on Lash Gorge Stratus's shoulder.

Because of you, he said.

Lash Gorge Stratus took a step back, not knowing how to respond. His breathing tightened. The alley where Yumi Malesca Couvreau's hut existed, the only one along that pathway, became brighter and clearer to Lash Gorge Stratus as he noticed every speck of dirt, each crevice and indentation along the concrete and against the stained, broken walls. The air—the smell of rotten vegetables and fruits mixed with freshly baked bread—was clear and strong. This is Dormier, he thought—my Dormier. He felt disgust for himself as he looked at Yumi Malesca Couvreau's eyes—gentle and welcoming with no scorn. Yumi Malesca Couvreau laughed.

Don't worry, he said. Your return is safe with me—I won't tell anyone. But if you do kill me, please give my regards to Alcee.

How did you know it's me? Lash Gorge Stratus said.

You've covered all of your body, and most of your face, he said, except your eyes. I see much in those eyes. Those eyes that once saved my life.

We were once all well, Lash Gorge Stratus said.

What happened to you? Yumi Malesca Couvreau asked.

Lash Gorge Stratus stood in a stupor—again, not knowing what to say, his eyes watery and transparent. He remained silent.

I understand, Yumi Malesca Couvreau said. The magma still lives.

Very much so, Lash Gorge Stratus said. My apologies. I

don't know what to say. I have no answer.

You should go back to the way you were, Yumi Malesca Couvreau said. Dormier was healthier back then, even the untouchables were happier then. But it's not my place to say.

Lash Gorge Stratus was having visions of when he was with his family. He and Alcee would walk to the untouchables to provide food and money to those they had made acquaintances with during the years. He remembered the conversation he had with his wife.

I wish we could feed and support all of the untouchables, Alcee had said.

Maybe we can, Leaus Perdu III replied.

They were walking toward the untouchables to meet Yumi Malesca Couvreau—they had promised him salmon, zucchini, and bread during the last time they had met.

Do you think it's possible? Alcee wondered.

Leaus Perdu III spoke with confidence.

My dear, he said. We will find a way. I've often envisioned a time when there was a way to support the poor.

Are you thinking about entering politics? Alcee said.

To help those in need of help, he said, would be my only reason to enter such activities.

Alcee took his hand and squeezed it tightly.

Lash Gorge Stratus felt a tap on his shoulder that broke his trance. He saw Yumi Malesca Couvreau standing before him, smiling.

You are here, he said.

He took his hand and put some coins in his palm.

Here, he said. Take this.

Lash Gorge Stratus looked at the coins in his hand. He looked at Yumi Malesca Couvreau and re-lived his history in a series of flashes that only lasted a moment. He took Yumi Malesca Couvreau's hand and put the coins back in his palm.

Take me to the untouchables, Lash Gorge Stratus said. Please.

$\text{A}\text{l}\text{e}\text{j}\text{o}$ had given Thuroon the following two days off to spend time with his family since the night they had dinner together. After such a pleasant night, and with the two days off, Thuroon was looking forward to going back to work for the first time since his first day working for Alejo.

As usual, he entered Alejo's mansion and went straight to work without seeking his master, as he knew not to interrupt his morning routine. He noticed that there wasn't much to clean and that there weren't too many chores to tackle, but he still found some work to do. When lunchtime came, Thuroon went to find Alejo to ask what he wanted for lunch. He didn't find him in the bedroom or in the library. He went out to the field to see if he was riding his newly acquired horse, but the field was empty.

Journey, Thuroon said.

He remembered that Alejo had mentioned that he was taking a trip during the night they had dinner together. He thought about the barn, thinking that maybe he was grooming his new horse. He entered the barn and breathed in the smell of hay and manure—closing his eyes, he heard the gentle breathing of the horse. He knelt down and felt the ground, running the dirt through his fingers, he felt at home.

Soft, clean dirt, Thuroon said.

He opened his eyes and saw Alejo hanging dead from the rafter of the barn. Thuroon closed his eyes and sighed before walking up to Alejo. He took an ax and climbed up three bales of hay. He cut Alejo down, the sound making a quiet thud upon the dirt of the barn. Thuroon jumped down from the bales of hay and shifted Alejo to where his head faced the ceiling. His body was heavy. He laid him down on the dirt and closed Alejo's eyes with his fingertips. Thuroon's own eyes were watery, and his body shook. On his knees, he lifted Alejo's head.

Sir, Thuroon pleaded. Sir.

Thuroon tapped his fingers against Alejo's cheeks.

Sir, Thuroon said. Lunch. What would you like to eat?

He ran his fingers through Alejo's neatly parted hair.

Sir, Thuroon said. Please.

He bowed his head and quietly cried to himself. He laid Alejo's body over his shoulders and went back to the mansion, taking him upstairs to his bed. Covered in sweat, Thuroon breathed hard as he positioned Alejo on the bed with his arms by his side. He fixed his hair and shirt and tie to make sure he looked nice as he lay dead. Once he finished, he took a deep breath and looked around the room. Without hesitation, he cleaned Alejo's room and all adjacent rooms. He cleaned the hallways and the rugs. He polished all that could be polished, and then he cleaned the living room, the kitchen, the study, all as hard as he could—the sweat pressed hard against his shirt and dripped steadily from his chin and forehead. When he finished, there was still daylight. He went upstairs to check on Alejo and found him looking peaceful. It was then, Thuroon realized, that he must report Alejo's death to the city officials.

Sir, Thuroon said. Sir. I am so sorry. I wish you the best.

After much walking and many distractions from the daily activities of Dormier, Vienna and her box of rats found themselves amongst the untouchables. As she walked down the street, all of her neighbors and acquaintances remained quiet—they wouldn't look at her but they knew that she was back.

But Vienna walked with her chin up and her rats were just as energetic. She walked to her mother's place, noticing the newly constructed hut. She found her mother sleeping on the hard concrete covered in a rug used as a blanket. Vienna was full of excitement, but she tried to stay quiet, as she didn't want to wake her mother. She lay beside her with her box of rats and kissed Sari on the forehead. She put her arms around her mother and closed her eyes, going to sleep as if she was just a child nestling with her mother years ago.

And just as it was years ago, during Vienna's childhood, she woke up to a swarm of kisses on her cheeks and forehead. She felt her mother's hand run through her hair. She heard Sari whispering to herself. She could feel her mother's tears against her face as Sari hugged her.

Mother, Vienna said.

I have mango juice, Sari said. And two potatoes. Please take them.

Vienna sat up. She could see that it was dark outside through the gap between the rug door and bamboo frame. She sat at the table but refused to eat unless Sari took a potato and some juice for herself. Sari gave in and ate one potato with her daughter; she only pretended to sip the mango juice as they caught up about their past adventures.

Where is Cirrus Stratus? Vienna said.

We are still in search, Sari said. I am to meet Alcee soon, when the sun comes up, to help her find him.

Do you think he's still alive? Vienna asked.

We both do, Sari said. Just as we both knew that you were still alive. Alcee laughed the other day saying that with all the chaos hovering over this town, Cirrus Stratus is somewhere out there, causing part of it.

I'm in love with someone I've never met, Vienna said. Someone who has caused such trouble for this town, someone I've never seen, yet I can't stop thinking about him.

My dear, Sari said, welcome home.

After Thuroon reported Alejo's death, his will and testament were revealed, which was recently updated, stating that Thuroon was to inherit Alejo's estate. The Ethicginian Party and its affiliating crew were in rage, claiming that Thuroon had murdered Alejo so that he could take over Alejo's assets. He was kidnapped shortly after and kept in the Ethicginian Party's headquarters as the organization demanded a change of the will and testament, transferring all inheritance to the party.

Stripped to the bare minimum and blindfolded, Thuroon was kept in the same room where Vienna was taken.

The city officials didn't suspect murder at all; before killing himself, Alejo specifically went to them asking for them to look after Thuroon and assist with the transition of the estate, an ominous hint that he might take his own life. Additionally, it could be proven that Thuroon was nowhere near Alejo during his time of death as he was at home with family and friends per witnesses.

The Ethicginian Party sent a note of ransom, stating a list of demands including the transfer of Alejo's estate to the party, the arrest and trial of Thuroon, and for additional funds to be given to the party by the city or Thuroon himself as they claimed that he was the one who killed Alejo, who was a great asset to the Ethicginian Party.

Lash Gorge Stratus, still following Yumi Malesca Couvreau to the untouchables, heard news on the streets about Alejo's death and Thuroon's kidnapping.

You must leave, Yumi Malesca Couvreau said.

I hope to see the untouchables soon, he said. But I must attend to some duties that require my attention.

You know what to do, Yumi Malesca Couvreau said. My friend, set this city as it was before.

Lash Gorge Stratus breathed in the streets of Dormier. He heard every sound—people, dogs, arguments, laughter, the sound of metal clanking. He heard it all.

I promise to come back, he said. I won't desert you as I did before.

You never left me, Yumi Malesca Couvreau said. I've only been waiting.

They parted ways. Lash Gorge Stratus, now reacquainted with his surroundings, walked toward the Ethicginian Party's headquarters. He thought about Alejo and regretted the path that he had influenced Alejo to take, becoming one of his mentors as he was one of the leaders of the Ethicginian Party. He enticed him to join the endeavors of the party.

He didn't look anyone in the eyes as he walked—some offered him coins and others cursed at him for being in the wrong area of town.

He ran his hands along the walls of the buildings he passed—the city was fully drenched in his blood and wrongdoing. Walking swiftly, he remembered when he and his family would go around town, helping the citizens of Dormier.

There was a sparrow flying not too far ahead of him. The sparrows of Dormier, he thought, the kites of this city. As he looked around, he saw a speckled town, covered in reds and yellows and blues and greens and purples.

This town of paint, Lash Gorge Stratus thought.

He saw the city in a different way—it was the way he saw it before joining the party, when he was Leaus Perdu III. The potential, the beauty, the hurt, the hard workers, the dreamers, the homeless—it all came back to him.

As he turned the corner, approaching the headquarters, he became overwhelmed with guilt. He thought about all the wrong he had done, both to people he knew and didn't know, including his own family. He had earned the reputation of being the most brutal killer of Dormier, though he, himself, had never killed anyone. He had gained this notoriety through the antics of those who worked for him, and he realized that it would haunt him for the rest of his life.

Please forgive me, Lash Gorge Stratus hoped.

He walked toward the headquarters, where he saw two men standing outside of the door. These men had been closely affiliated with Lash Gorge Stratus during his reign—his henchmen, his servants. They recognized Lash Gorge Stratus immediately, despite his face being covered up.

Both Whale Ley and Jomiah started to shout in celebration with the return of their leader. They ran up to him and hugged him, patted him on the shoulders, and shook his hand.

Welcome home, Jomiah said.

We missed you, Whale Ley said. Now we will be back in full control.

Lash Gorge Stratus didn't return their excitement.

Alejo, he said. His servant—Thuroon, is he inside?

Whale Ley howled, lifting his face up to the sky.

We have him, he said. We have him inside. He did wrong, and we have him.

We will do what you want us to do with him, Jomiah said. Maybe drowning his head until he confesses? We'll give him our own trial.

I'll go inside and hear what he has to say, Lash Gorge Stratus said.

Welcome home, Whale Ley said.

Lash Gorge Stratus nodded his head and walked in, immediately feeling both dizzy and guilty. He passed by more of his cohorts, all of whom he recognized. They hugged him vigorously and welcomed him home.

Lash Gorge Stratus kept quiet. He wasn't sure how to react, knowing that he no longer wanted to be a part of the Ethicginian Party. He nodded.

Where is Thuroon? he asked.

The usual room, one of the men said.

Allow me, then, Lash Gorge Stratus said.

He walked through the small crowd, went down the hallway and entered the room, still overwhelmed with shame for all that had taken place in this room—including the kidnapping of Vienna and keeping her in such a horrible state.

He saw Thuroon—blindfolded, his hands and feet tied. He could see tears coming down from underneath the rag covering his eyes.

Thuroon, Lash Gorge Stratus said.

Thuroon sniffed and took a deep breath.

Sir, he said. I am here.

Lash Gorge Stratus laughed.

I am no sir, he said. I'm Lash Gorge Stratus.

Oh dear, Thuroon said. Are you going to kill me?

Lash Gorge Stratus lowered his head.

No, he said. I am not going to kill you.

I didn't kill Alejo, Thuroon said.

I understand, Lash Gorge Stratus said. What do you think happened to him?

He killed himself, Thuroon said. Honestly. I had nothing to do with it. I served him, and that was all I could do.

I am here to help, Lash Gorge Stratus said.

Thuroon sniffled again.

Why aren't you going to kill me?

I am not the one to do so, he said. I know you're innocent.

I just want to be dead, Thuroon said. Or back at home with my family. But I don't want to be kept like this.

I understand, Lash Gorge Stratus said. I will find a way for you to get out of here.

Sir, Thuroon said. Thank you, sir. But if it doesn't happen, please have someone look after my family.

I promise, Lash Gorge Stratus said. But you'll be the one to take care of them. You will see them again.

The door opened and in walked Abliss Rang, the main leader of the Ethicginian Party. He had left Dormier for quite some time to take care of affairs overseas—to spread his control and power—and had left Lash Gorge Stratus as the director of the party while he was away. He smiled.

Welcome back, Abliss Rang said. I knew you'd be back. I was never worried.

Thuroon needs to be let go, Lash Gorge Stratus said.

Abliss Rang cackled and then abruptly stopped laughing.

No, he said. Do you realize the power we have here now? With having him here, we are in complete control.

Sir, Thuroon said, his lips quivering.

Quiet, Abliss Rang said. Do not speak unless you are spoken to, unless I tell you to speak.

He's no murderer, Lash Gorge Stratus said. Think of his family as you would think of your own family.

What is this? Abliss Rang said.

He pulled out a cigar and lit it, puff after puff, blowing the smoke in rings toward Lash Gorge Stratus.

You've changed, Abliss Rang noticed, haven't you?

Just trying to do right, he said.

Well maybe you should join this man, Abliss Rang said. That feels right.

Lash Gorge tensed his body in case Abliss Rang tried to attack him. He knew he could defeat him; however, if more of his men came, he would be in much trouble. He looked around and saw a metal pipe in the corner of the room.

Do you have an alternative idea? Lash Gorge Stratus said.

Abliss Rang puffed his cigar with both hands in his pocket—his cigar never leaving his mouth, he spoke with one eye squinting from the smoke.

Return to us, he said, and there's no trouble. But you've lost my trust, a trust you will have to earn again.

Lash Gorge Stratus spat.

How about a duel, he said. If I win, Thuroon is free. If you win, I am at your will.

Just as Abliss Rang was about to speak, the door opened and in walked Whale Ley and Jomiah, holding Sari and Alcee in custody—revolvers to their backs.

We found them trying to break in, Whaley Ley said.

Yes, Abliss Rang said. Of course.

Lash Gorge Stratus and Alcee looked at each other. It was a look they hadn't given each other since they were together as a family.

Dear, Lash Gorge Stratus said.

Dear, Alcee replied.

Well, Abliss Rang said. Would you like to join them?

Lash Gorge Stratus ignored him and continued to look into Alcee's eyes.

I'll take that as a yes, Abliss Rang said.

He looked at Whaley Ley.

After you tie them up, he said. Tie him up as well. Our control has just grown, and he is of no use to us anymore.

But sir, Whaley Ley said.

Do as I say, Abliss Rang said.

Lash Gorge Stratus remained silent, only looking at his wife. Both Alcee and Sari were kicked in the back of their legs, causing them to fall down to their knees. Their captors began to tie them up.

The eyes? Jomiah asked.

Cover them, Abliss Rang said.

Lash Gorge Stratus gritted his teeth.

Dear, Lash Gorge Stratus said.

Despite struggling and being roughed around, she spoke.

Dear, Alcee said.

I'm tired, Lash Gorge Stratus said. Let's go home.

Let's go home, dear, Alcee said.

Abliss Rang laughed and Lash Gorge Stratus was struck behind the head, but he didn't fall. He turned around and faced Whale Ley.

Sorry, Whale Ley said. Just following orders.

Try harder, Lash Gorge Stratus said.

Whale Ley struck his face. Lash Gorge Stratus stood still, a cut on his cheek formed, a thin line of blood dripped down his face.

Come on, Lash Gorge Stratus said. I've taught you better.

Yes sir, Whale Ley said.

He struck him again, and still, there wasn't an effective result. Abliss Rang threw his cigar at Whale Ley in frustration and looked at Jomiah. Both Whale Ley and Jomiah proceeded to hit Lash Gorge Stratus, who remained standing while not resisting their blows. Whale Ley and Jomiah stopped, breathing hard.

Dear, Lash Gorge Stratus said.

He was covered in blood—his face puffed, and bruises already started to form.

I'm sorry, he said. I've made too many mistakes.

Alcee, blindfolded and tied, couldn't help but to smile.

You were always a wonderful dancer, she said.

Without hesitation, and as Whale Ley and Jomiah were resting, he grabbed each of them by the neck and pushed them against the concrete wall, knocking both of them out. As he turned around, he saw Abliss Rang holding the pipe, swinging it toward him and landing on his shoulder. Lash Gorge Stratus fell to his knees—he was struck again on the back, and fell full force to the ground.

$Just$ before Sari and Alcee had left for the headquarters, Sari had asked Vienna to take care of some errands. She finished, and for the rest of the day, she couldn't find her mother. Worried, she knew in her gut that her mother went to the Ethicginian Party's headquarters to help Alcee find her son. She looked around the hut and saw some spare bamboo sticks—she picked up three pieces to use for protection and went off to find her mother and Alcee.

When she arrived, Whale Ley and Jomiah were standing outside of the door, continuing to watch their post.

Well well well, Jomiah said. Look who it is.

Whale Ley spat and cackled.

If it isn't the pretty lady herself, he said. The town's princess.

And look, Jomiah said. She's got weapons, too.

I'm here to do no harm, Vienna said. I'm looking for my mother.

Much too bold to come here, Whale Ley said.

This is a peaceful visit, Vienna said.

Then why the bamboo? Jomiah asked.

This is not for you all, she said. I take it everywhere I go, just for general protection.

Such a mighty princess, Jomiah mocked.

Maybe you're going to need it, Whale Ley said.

Please, Vienna said. Is my mother here?

The evening sun started to show between the clouds, glittered with hawks looping around in the sky. There was an uneasy silence filling the town—the only sounds were that of insects and stray cats. The heat was settling down upon their shoulders, and the sweat came down.

She's here, Whale Ley said. She sure is here.

May I see her? Vienna asked.

Sure can, Jomiah said. We'll take you inside.

Go ahead and put that bamboo down, Whale Ley said.

Vienna tossed them aside and followed them indoors, knowing full well she had been captured again. She just wanted to see her mother. Flashbacks of when she was kept there against her will flickered in her mind.

This should all look familiar to you, Whale Ley said.

Both he and Jomiah laughed. Vienna maintained her kindness.

And here I am again, she said.

She recognized the hallway and the main room from when she escaped the headquarters. She drew a deep breath, thinking of her box of rats, which she kept safely hidden in her hut. She recognized the door at the end of the hallway, which Jomiah opened.

After you, he said.

Vienna knew she wasn't going to be let go—that she would be kept by them again, but it was most important to see her mother alive. She walked in and saw the four tied and blindfolded, sitting against the wall. She saw Sari.

Mother, Vienna said.

Vienna, Sari said. Leave at once. Tell the city officials. Tell everyone you can.

It's too late for that now, Whale Ley said. I'm sure you all would love to sit and talk. I'm afraid we're all out of tea.

Jomiah cackled.

Before Vienna could speak, she was grabbed and tied. Jomiah's face was the last thing she saw before being blindfolded. She joined the four, sitting down and leaning her back against the wall, having more flashbacks of her previous kidnapping. She wondered why she had seen Lash Gorge Stratus sitting next to her mother and Alcee when she first entered the room.

Why is he here? Vienna asked.

Who? Sari said.

The man of evil, she said.

It seems that he has gone through too much, Alcee said. Perhaps he is back with us.

Lash Gorge Stratus remained silent.

And who is the other gentleman? she went on.

Good miss, Thuroon said. I am Thuroon. The reason why you all are here. I'm sorry.

No apologies needed, Vienna said. We are all here together.

We will leave here alive, Lash Gorge Stratus said. If I know my son, we will all be well.

Cirrus

Stratus peered through the bushes and looked out to the Ethicginian Party's headquarters. He saw Whale Ley and Jomiah sitting on the stoop in front of the building, spitting tobacco. He walked around the building, hiding behind bushes and trees to survey the area. He didn't see anyone else. Two men, he thought. I could beat them. But he was worried about the noise it would make, alerting the others.

He reached the other side, directly across from where he was first located. He saw the bamboo sticks that Vienna had to leave behind before going inside. He picked up two large stones and started to run toward them. The two men didn't notice him; they were looking straight ahead as they talked to each other, ignoring whatever was to the sides of them. In one single motion, he threw the rocks at them, hitting both of them in the shoulders, while picking up the bamboo sticks. By the time they realized what was happening, Cirrus Stratus was standing in front of them—he swung the sticks at them until they fell to the ground. He jumped on the two and started punching until they were unconscious. He spat and looked around, seeing no one else. The two men were dragged back into the bushes and tied with vines from a nearby tree. Cirrus Stratus took his shirt off and tore it into pieces to gag each of them. He spat.

Just before the stoop of the house was a peacock—blue and green and yellow, and its head held high. From a tree just beyond the peacock came a loud, crisp and clear chirp. Perched on a branch was a bluebird.

Cirrus Stratus took another rock and ran to throw it at the door of the large house. After, he sprinted back and hid behind the bushes, waiting. He looked up at the bluebird and started to whistle along with it. The peacock stood in front of the door, its head moving side to side and back and forth. The door opened and two men walked outside—Roter and Laurez.

What's this? Laurez wondered.

Looks like food, Roter said.

Say, Laurez said. Where'd Whale Ley and Jomiah go?

They probably went to the saloon, Roter answered.

Always slacking off, Laurez said.

Cirrus Stratus took a deep breath—his chest stuck out as he held it in for a moment before exhaling. He picked up a rock and threw it at the feet of the peacock, startling it. In its frightened state, the peacock became defensive and started attacking the two men, spreading its wings and using its beak to peck at whatever it could peck at—head, neck, shoulder, chest. The two men started shouting and cursing, running around in circles. As the peacock had positioned itself between the men and the door of the headquarters, they were forced to retreat into the woods for protection. Cirrus Stratus smiled as the men ran away. He eased toward the peacock and it looked at him with a tilted head. Cirrus Stratus tilted his head, too, and couldn't help but to smile again.

Thank you, he said.

The peacock shook its head and walked away into the woods. Cirrus Stratus opened the front door, slowly, quietly, and peered in—no one was around. He walked in and saw the hallway and hoped that this was the path to find his father, or perhaps his mother or Vienna. But he didn't enter it immediately. He found the kitchen first, and looked for items that could start a fire. He found gasoline.

The ground shook.

Cirrus Stratus started a fire and looked around. He had felt the ground shake once before when he was a child, and this was the first time it had happened since then.

The captured—Thuroon, Vienna, Sari, Alcee, and Lash Gorge Stratus—also felt the ground shake. Lash Gorge Stratus laughed.

I was wondering, he said. It has been quite a while.

He thought about the last time the earth shook—he was with his son, digging for bones and gems.

This land is unhappy, Alcee said.

It could be a reckoning, Lash Gorge Stratus said.

The ground shook again, causing the group to fall to their sides. Vienna couldn't help but to laugh, leading everyone else to laugh as well.

We will be okay, Lash Gorge Stratus said. If Cirrus Stratus does not save us, the earth will.

You seem quite sure that your son will be here to help us, Sari said.

I am, he said. For I sense a feeling of unrest amongst the Ethicginian Party. There's this feeling of chaos, and Cirrus Stratus has the ability, more than anyone else, to affect them this way.

Just as he finished speaking, there was a series of loud noises, shouting and clashing. And then there was silence. The door opened, and Alcee and Lash Gorge Stratus heard a recognizable voice.

Mother, Cirrus Stratus said.

Alcee controlled her excitement with a big smile, tears ran down her face for the first time in years.

My son, she said.

Cirrus Stratus walked toward them and untied his mother first. She kissed him on the cheek and they gave each other a strong embrace.

I missed you, Cirrus Stratus said. But we will catch up later.

He untied Sari and then went on to Vienna. Without rushing, with softness, he untied Vienna, keeping the blindfold in his hand, he was speechless at first. Vienna was trying to get her sight back, her eyes still adjusting to the light.

Hi, she said.

I am Cirrus Stratus, he said.

So nice to meet you, Vienna said.

Cirrus Stratus wiped his hands on his pants and stuck them out for Vienna to grab. He pulled her up, trying to speak, but no words appeared. All he could do was smile while looking into her eyes. This was the first time he was this close to the lady he loved but never spoke to. He managed to talk.

We are here, he said. And this is wonderful.

Vienna, with wide eyes and her head tilted, and her hands still clasped with Cirrus Stratus, found herself lost. She looked at his bare body—the muscles around his chest, the thin stomach, and tightly packed biceps.

So you are the reason why Dormier has awoken, she said.

The ground trembled, causing the remaining two to fall over again, and Cirrus Stratus stumbled into Vienna's body.

It's been quite a day, Cirrus Stratus said.

He suddenly remembered that there were still more people to free. He looked around and saw Thuroon and Lash Gorge Stratus.

Why is he here? he asked.

My dear, Alcee said, he's trying hard to make amends—your father, my husband.

I don't know what to do about this, Cirrus Stratus said.

You've been given many chances, Alcee said.

He knew what his mother meant and went to his father to free him without saying a word. He took off his blindfold, and Lash Gorge Stratus blinked repeatedly, adjusting his eyesight.

Son, he said.

Who are you? Cirrus Stratus said.

His fists were clenched, but his eyes were watery and revealing.

I'm here for you and your mother, he said.

Why? Cirrus Stratus asked.

Because I was lost, Lash Gorge Stratus said, and your mother helped me to be found.

Cirrus Stratus, not knowing what to do, didn't reply and went to help Vienna untie Thuroon. The ground shook again. Thuroon, now free, stuck out his hand to greet Cirrus Stratus.

I am Thuroon.

And I am Cirrus Stratus.

You work for Alejo? he asked.

No longer, for he is dead, Thuroon said.

This was the first that Cirrus Stratus heard of this news and he didn't have time to fully comprehend it, as the door opened and Abliss Rang walked in with a few of his men, coughing. Smoke could be seen behind them.

Cirrus Stratus's eyes widened and he jumped up and down in excitement, knowing that he would get to fight Abliss Rang and his men. Without saying a word, he ran to his opponents and started throwing fists, but the fight didn't last too long. The ground shook again, causing the building to cave in—the ceiling fell and the ground opened. Abliss Rang didn't roll into the hole, but most of his men did. Thuroon was falling into the giant hole in the earth, but he caught hold of the edge, barely hanging between the realms of life and death. As the others wrestled to gain stability, Cirrus Stratus ran to help Thuroon.

Please, Thuroon said, look after my family.

Cirrus Stratus, still completely calm, smiled and spoke.

You will have dinner with them tomorrow night, he said. I assure you.

He pulled Thuroon from the edge, onto the floor. The structure of the building continued to crumble, and the hole in the ground shook again. This time, Abliss Rang's men fell into the chasm. Abliss Rang, losing his grip, was grabbing on to the ledge with both of his hands as tightly as he could. He was smiling and laughing. Cirrus Stratus watched his father walk toward him as the sides of the room began to cave in. The noises and the clashes caused Thuroon and Sari to hug each other for comfort. Abliss Rang looked at Lash Gorge Stratus standing above him.

I would rather die before receiving any help from you, Abliss Rang said.

I never said I'd help you, Lash Gorge Stratus said.

I'm disappointed in you, Abliss Rang said.

I understand, Lash Gorge Stratus said, but that means nothing to me.

Abliss Rang started to cackle.

You could have had it all.

I would rather have nothing, Lash Gorge Stratus said.

He stood still and watched Abliss Rang's grip loosen. He continued to cackle and smile as he let go of the edge and Lash Gorge Stratus watched him fall into the darkness. Cirrus Stratus walked over and put his hand on his father's shoulder.

Father, he said.

Lash Gorge Stratus turned his head and put his hand on top of his son's hand.

We need to go, Cirrus Stratus said.

Lash Gorge Stratus didn't know how to respond—he was surprised by his son's amity.

Let's go, Cirrus Stratus said. The world is about to fall.

My son—Lash Gorge Stratus began.

He was about to apologize, but before he could say anything, his son interrupted him.

No time, he said. Protect the gang, and I will protect you all.

Lash Gorge Stratus looked around and saw Alcee, Thuroon, Sari, Vienna recovering from the broken ground. The building shook, and smoke was coming in heavily. He ran to the group, urging them to exit as the structure continued to break. The doorway started to cave in and Lash Gorge Stratus dashed straight into it, letting the upper end of the doorway rest on his back, keeping the exit open.

Go, he said. Go.

The gang ran out—all except Cirrus Stratus and Alcee.

Leave, Cirrus Stratus said. Go. We'll catch up.

Alcee kissed her son on the cheek and looked at her husband, who looked at her the same way he looked at her when he saw Alcee singing in the ocean.

Run, mother, Cirrus Stratus said.

She took off as the building continued to crack and crumble. Cirrus Stratus remained calm. Despite the chaos and danger, he walked to his father, who was still in the middle of the doorway.

Go, Lash Gorge Stratus said. Follow your mother. Take care of her.

Looking at the pressure upon Lash Gorge Stratus's shoulders and back, Cirrus Stratus knew that it would be difficult for his father to escape without being buried by the rubble. The ground shook again and as Cirrus Stratus looked at his father, he remembered moments of his parents dancing and twirling around the living room during the soirees at home.

Please, son, Lash Gorge Stratus said.

Clouds of dark smoke filled the room, but in between the billows, Cirrus Stratus saw his father, vividly, clearly. He remembered holding his father's hand, and the kisses on his forehead, and flying kites. Cirrus Stratus grinned and pushed his father through the doorway to the other side. As the structure began to topple, he saw his father looking at him with watery eyes. Cirrus Stratus continued to smile as his father shouted his name.

Father, Cirrus Stratus said.

And then there was nothing as the room fell apart.

Alcee, Lash Gorge Stratus, Vienna, Sari, and Thuroon stood outside of the Ethicginian Party's headquarters, watching it being destroyed. They were happy that their enemies' foundation was no longer, but more than that they were overwhelmed with sadness, not knowing if Cirrus Stratus was alive.

He just smiled and pushed me, Lash Gorge Stratus said. There was nothing I could do.

They all remained hopeful, and after the building had finished crumbling they ventured into the broken pieces to find Cirrus Stratus. They called his name, but the fire was too strong for the group to enter the area where Cirrus Stratus was last seen. There wasn't much they could do but retreat with their mouths and noses covered. Lash Gorge Stratus remained confident.

I truly believe he's still around, he said.

I believe so too, Vienna said.

With the destruction of the Ethicginian Party's headquarters, the death of Abliss Rang, and the rebirth of Leaus Perdu III, Dormier was born again and thriving. The multiple earthquakes had caused some damage and threatened the possibility of another volcano eruption, but once the initial shock subsided, the town began to rebuild with freedom and relief. No one was scared anymore.

Leaus Perdu III and Alcee moved back to their former house, patiently waiting for Cirrus Stratus to return, and despite the rumors that certain inhabitants had seen Cirrus Stratus's ghost, the couple remained hopeful that he was not a specter. Thuroon became one of their assistants and adjusted well to his new life, knowing that he would be able to take care of his family without any stress.

Alcee and Leaus Perdu III had offered Sari and Vienna a place to stay, and though humbled with the proposition, they politely declined.

So kind of you, and we are forever grateful for the offer, Sari said, but we will be fine.

Sari went on to explain that being an untouchable wasn't a burden, but rather a way of life. And through work, they would find a better living opportunity on their own.

It is our own process, Sari said.

Vienna helped her mother with tasks and work, but her mind remained with Cirrus Stratus, wondering if she would ever see him again, dead or alive.

As the rebirth of Dormier was happening, there came the birth of new businesses, including cuisine. However, one particular business was a mystery. Every Sunday, the untouchables would find a meal at their huts in the morning. The untouchables had no clue where it came from, but they ate the food, wrapped in brown paper, with great fervor. The news of such delicious food had spread around town, leading the rest of the population over to the untouchables to see what was behind the great aroma that sauntered throughout the town. The untouchables were kind and giving, sharing their food with the rest, believing that all should try such a wonderful meal.

The town fell in love with the mystery dish, but no one knew where to find the place that provided the meal; however, soon enough, random houses would find the paper wrapped food at their doorsteps in the mornings on random days, including the house of Alcee and Lash Gorge Stratus.

One night, as the couple stayed up late conversing and drinking shandy, they heard a noise outside of their door.

That must be the cook, Alcee said.

Let's follow him, Leaus Perdu III said.

They kept their distance as they followed the figure, who held two large baskets, going to random houses and dropping off packages. It was well into the night when they followed the shadow out of the volcano to a small hut just outside the edges of the Dormier. It was tucked away against a wall of rock, hidden from sight.

Now we know, Leaus Perdu III said.

Let's come back tomorrow and give this person a visit, Alcee said. We'll bring Sari and Vienna, too.

If they hadn't seen where the hut existed, Leaus Perdu III and Alcee wouldn't have known where to look even during the daytime.

I'm so excited, Vienna said. We must know who cooks such a delicious meal.

They walked up to the hut and Leaus Perdu III said hello. He said it again, and they heard some rustling inside and the rug door was pushed aside.

Oh dear, Alcee said. My son.

Hello, Cirrus Stratus said. Are you in need of some help?

Son, Leaus Perdu III said. We all knew that you were still alive.

They walked toward Cirrus Stratus to hug him, but he backed off, not letting the couple touch him.

I apologize, Cirrus Stratus said. You must be confused with someone else.

Vienna pulled her mother aside.

It is his ghost, Vienna said.

It's us, Alcee said. Your parents—we can never forget our son.

I'm sorry, he said. But I don't recognize you—maybe I look like your son.

You are Cirrus Stratus, Leaus Perdu III said.

To be honest, he said. I can't remember my name. However, I call myself Jamal Archangel III.

Aside, Leaus Perdu III whispered to Alcee, saying that

he must have amnesia, perhaps from an injury caused from the crumbling building.

He may have hit his head, Alcee said. We must help him to remember.

Vienna walked up to Cirrus Stratus, who, upon seeing her, immediately fixed his hair, and tucked his dirt-stained shirt into his hole-ridden pants.

Good lady, Cirrus Stratus said.

His eyes were large and round—in awe, just as they had always been when he saw Vienna, whether he recognized her or not.

I'm Vienna, she said.

So nice to meet you, Cirrus Stratus said. I am Jamal Archangel III.

Do you remember me? she asked.

I'm afraid I don't, he said. But I wish I did.

You wrote me a letter once, she said. And you killed two horses for me as a gift.

How are you so pretty? Cirrus Stratus asked.

Vienna didn't know how to reply and looked at her mother, who walked up to Cirrus Stratus.

What are these delicious meals you've been preparing? Sari said.

Alcee and Leaus Perdu III were still standing aside, talking to each other. Alcee had tears coming down her face, tears of both joy and despair.

He'll come back, Leaus Perdu III said. Don't worry.

Dormier is absolutely in love with your cooking, Sari said.

Thank you so much for asking, Cirrus Stratus said. I call them po'boys.

Po'boys, Vienna said.

Basically, a type of meat trapped between hardened bread, Cirrus Stratus said. And cheese.

So lovely, Vienna said.

Please tell me, Cirrus Stratus said. Did I know you before my memory was taken away?

You did, she said.

She walked up to him and embraced him. Cirrus Stratus felt enlightened.

I wish I could remember you all, he said.

Leaus Perdu III stepped toward him.

It will happen, he said. I promise.

Cirrus Stratus stared into each of their eyes, but no memories arrived. Alcee was determined. She whispered into his ear. So did his father. Vienna, and Sari, too. He listened intently, but none of their softened words led to any clarity.

I wish, Cirrus Stratus said.

So what different kinds do you make? Vienna said.

Pork sausage, ham, and roast beef, Cirrus Stratus said. All with cheese. But I would like to start including some kind of food from the sea as well.

It's wonderful, Sari said. How did you come up with this?

Cirrus Stratus explained that he woke up in the middle of nowhere, at night, not knowing what happened to him— all memory was lost, but he was starving. He had found some stale bread and for survival, killed a pig and cooked it. He put the meat between the stale bread and it tasted so good that he kept making the sandwich and started experimenting with different kinds of meats while living on the outskirts of the volcano. He had tried it with regular bread once, but it didn't taste the same, so he cooked the bread to give it some kind of crunch. In need of making money, he started to drop it off at various places to raise some attention, and he was just thinking of going into town and selling it for money.

I'm a poor boy, he said.

A wonderful idea, Leaus Perdu III said. You will do well with this.

Please, Alcee said. Come stay with us. Maybe that will help you.

But I have business to tend to, he said.

Of course, Leaus Perdu III said. We have plenty of room to use at home, and it will be more convenient to deliver your po'boys.

And it will be much more convenient for you if you work and stay at our house, Alcee said. Please.

Po'boys, Cirrus Stratus said.

A fortnight had passed since Cirrus Stratus had moved back to his parents' house. His po'boys were selling well. Everyone in Dormier had been eating them. Though Cirrus Stratus never charged the untouchables, they found other ways to repay him, giving him cooking equipment or crafts they made for their own living—much like Cirrus Stratus had done before.

Dormier had changed from despair and fear to sausage po'boys and laughter. The energy was like no other, and Cirrus Stratus's sandwiches had brought the town to a new unknown sensation of delight.

Vienna visited Cirrus Stratus every day since he moved back home, and every time, they would talk to each other with large round eyes, in constant awe of each other. His memory still hadn't come back, but he was enamored with Vienna just as much as he was before he lost his memory.

Though Sari and Vienna continued to live with the untouchables, they would visit Alcee and Leaus Perdu III quite frequently. They would attend their soirees, which in turn, helped Sari's business as a seamstress. Cirrus Stratus would make gourmet po'boys, constantly in search of the perfect taste and combination. His favorite was sausage and egg.

One morning after a soiree, Leaus Perdu III wanted to make breakfast for his family. He walked into Cirrus Stratus's room, which was full of all kinds of ornaments given to him by the untouchables.

Come, he said. I will make breakfast for you and Mother. Let's eat.

I'll be there in just a bit, Cirrus Stratus said. I just want to finish cleaning this floor. That way, Thuroon won't have to worry about it.

He was on his hands and knees, scrubbing the floor, making sure to cover each crack and crevice. He found peace—a sense of meditation in this action, and cleaned not only his room, but the whole house.

This way, he continued, Thuroon can have the day off.

He went back to his room, remembering that he wanted to clean under his bed frame—he found a piece of string and pulled on it, realizing that it was tied to a larger object. He pulled it out from under the bed.

Kite, he said.

He closed his eyes and had a series of visions—flying a kite with his father, eating outside with his mother. He saw two dead horses and Vienna in a white gown. He saw his own ghost. Cirrus Stratus opened his eyes and walked to the kitchen where his parents sat at the table. He smiled.

Mother, he said. Father.

You remember, Alcee said.

I'll be right back, Cirrus Stratus said. Please forgive me, but I'll be back.

Of course, son, Leaus Perdu III said. We will wait for you.

He put his arm around Alcee. Cirrus Stratus went back to his room to change before leaving the house. He wore a suit and tie and held a bouquet of flowers in one hand and a neatly wrapped po'boy in the other. He stood outside of Sari and Vienna's hut.

Vienna, he said.

He called her name a few times before she pushed aside the rug door—she had been grooming her rats. Before looking at Vienna, he saw the rats on a table huddled around a piece of cheese. They stopped eating and lifted their heads, looking at Cirrus Stratus.

Cirrus Stratus, she said. You look nice.

I dressed up for you, he said. Here.

He handed her the flowers and the po'boy.

I remember, he said.

You do? Vienna asked.

And I have seen the future, Cirrus Stratus said. And we are there.

They kissed—never letting go of each other for the rest of their lives, and in the future—the future that Cirrus Stratus had seen, there was a kite and it soared above the evening sun.

Thank You

Cirrus Stratus couldn't have been created without the support, love, and care of the following lovely beings:

Thank you to my friends, who without hesitation, have always shown so much kindness and support—your friendship means so much, truly and sincerely.

Thank you, Rien Fertel for being there, always. Thank you, Mike Bourgeois and Andy LeGoullon—thank you so much, for everything. Thank you, Chad and Bianca Cosby. Thank you, Karl Schott and Mandy Migues. Thank you, Andy Breaux. Thank you, Stacey Grow. Thank you, Luke Sonnier. Thank you, Patrick O'Neil. Thank you, Jerome Moroux. Thank you, Katie Culbert. Thank you, Story Frantzen and Jacob Camden. Thank you, Sara Lippmann. Thank you so much, Kyleigh McPhillips, for your guidance with this novel. Thank you, Lafayette Barnes & Noble. Thank you, Strangers.

Many thanks to the Literary Community who has provided so much encouragement.

Thank you, Spuyten Duyvil—for all of this.

And to my parents, Sarmistha and Subrata Dasgupta, my brother, Deep and my sister-in-law, Heidi—I love you all so much.

Shome Dasgupta is the author of ten books, including *The Seagull And The Urn* (HarperCollins India), *Spectacles* (Word West Press), *i am here And You Are Gone* (Winner of the 2010 OW Press Fiction Contest), *Anklet And Other Stories* (Golden Antelope Press), and a poetry collection, *Iron Oxide* (Assure Press). Forthcoming novels *Tentacles Numbing* (Thirty West) and *The Muu-Antiques* (Malarkey Books). His writing has appeared in *McSweeney's Internet Tendency*, *Hobart*, *New Orleans Review*, *X-R-A-Y*, *American Book Review*, *New Delta Review*, *Magma Poetry*, and elsewhere. His fiction and poetry have been anthologized in *Best Small Fictions 2019* and *Best Small Fictions 2021* (Sonder Press), *The &Now Awards 2: The Best Innovative Writing* (&Now Books), and *Poetic Voices Without Borders 2* (Gival Press). His work has been featured as a *storySouth* Million Writers Award Notable Story, and his stories and poems have been nominated for the Pushcart Prize, Best Small Fictions, Best Microfiction, Best Of The Net, and the Orison Anthology. He is the series editor of the *Wigleaf* Top 50. He lives in Lafayette, LA and can be found at www.shomedome.com and @laughingyeti.